A DRILL INSTRUCTOR'S JOURNEY

A DRILL INSTRUCTOR'S JOURNEY

LARRY ALLEN MCNAIR, SR.

CITIOFBOOKS, INC.
3736 Eubank NE Suite A1
Albuquerque, NM 87111-3579
www.citiofbooks.com
Hotline: 1 (877) 389-2759
Fax: 1 (505) 930-7244

Ordering Information:
Quantity sales. Special discounts are available on quantity purchases by corporations, associations, and others. For details, contact the publisher at the address above.

Printed in the United States of America.

ISBN-13:   Softcover   978-1-962366-68-7
        eBook   978-1-962366-69-4

Library of Congress Control Number: 2023919948

TABLE OF CONTENTS

I d edicate this book to my lovely wife Teresa H. McNair. We got married on December 29, 1974. I give her the credit for my career. Terri took care of our children Larry, Corey, and Kristi. She has been a blessing sent by God. Terri has been my best friend I love you very much.

WHERE THE JOURNEY BEGINS

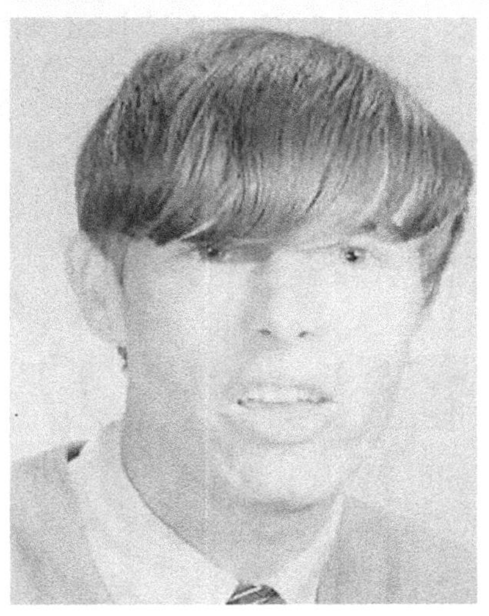

It was November 8th, 1970 and I was on a Greyhound bus going to Raleigh, North Carolina. Once I arrived in Raleigh, I went straight to my hotel, the YMCA, and checked in. It was late in the evening, so I used one of my food vouchers to eat supper. After finishing supper, I went back to my room, but I did not sleep well that night. My mind was on the things I would be doing at the Military Entrance Processing center (MEPS) the following day.

I was 17 years old, eight days from my 18th birthday. I was on my way to be a Marine. I grew up in a small community called Shallotte,

North Carolina, about 2 hours from Camp Lejeune. Growing up around Shallotte was such a blessing. Some of my best memories happened at Shallotte High School.

The following day, I was up early. I got dressed and I was off to breakfast. After breakfast, I went to the MEPS. The first thing they had us do was take the ASVAB. The test would determine what job the Marine Corps would assign us. Then they had us strip down to our underwear. The doctors and Corpsmen checked everything. They told me I was in excellent health. After lunch we took the oath of enlistment.

Then I was on my way to the Raleigh Airport. It was time to board the airplane, and before I knew it, the plane landed in Charleston, South Carolina. A Marine Gunnery Sergeant met us. He was there to make sure we got on the bus to Parris Island and behaved ourselves. We were joking around and just having fun. The Gunnery Sergeant informed us that our world was about to change, but his words went in one ear and out the other.

It was time to board the Greyhound bus for Parris Island. The Gunnery Sergeant gave us a fine farewell, and we were off. Everyone on the bus was nervous, but we tried to keep our minds clear. Once we got close to Parris Island, the bus driver told us to sit up straight and keep our mouths shut. We could see the main gate, and you could hear a pin drop. The military policeman gave permission for the bus to enter the base.

We arrived at the Receiving Barracks. The Drill Instructor ordered us off the bus. He actually told us to get off the damn bus. "Recruits, put your feet on the yellow footprints! Your mouth will be shut unless the Recruit is asked a question. Faster! Faster! Faster! Freeze your body!" Now we knew he was a Drill Instructor. The Drill Instructor took us into the Receiving Barracks.

Now, a life-changing moment was about to happen. We were in three separate lines. Three older men were standing behind barber chairs, laugh- ing their asses off. We knew what was going to happen. Well, it happened quickly. We were the long hair generation, but not any longer. We became blooming idiots without our hair. Like Samson of the Old Testament, he lost his strength. We lost the ability to think for ourselves.

Back in the receiving barracks, we were now standing at a table. The Drill Instructor gave each one of us a number and told us to count off. That became a disaster that we could not get right. Finally, a miracle happened! We were able to count starting with one. After we had counted off, we had to empty our pockets. The Drill Instructor checked everything. What he deemed not important was put in a shit can (trash can).

Next, we stripped down to our underwear. We learned to call them skivvies. Our civilian clothes were boxed up and we would not see them again until we graduated. The Drill Instructor started to issue us uniforms. He issued four sets of green sateen, six White t-shirts, six skivvies, four pairs of green socks, three green covers (hats) and two pairs of black boots. The Drill Instructor taught us how to wear the uniform. He checked every one of us in our uniform. By this point, it was about 0400.

The Drill Instructor took us to a barracks in the same building. We were in front of stacked beds, which we later learned to call racks. We counted off again and made the same stupid mistakes. Finally, we got it right again. We were told to get in the rack. Before we knew it, we were up again. It was 0600, November 10th, 1970. The Drill Instructor got us dressed again by the numbers. Socks, trousers, blouses, and boots. Then we were outside standing on the yellow footprints. We were told to face to the right. You would not believe how many rights there were! We were all dumbasses! Well, we were finally off to the mess hall. This was our first time eating in a Marine mess hall. Somehow, we got in and moved down the mess line sideways with a mess tray. It was the first time I saw anything like it.

The food that we were going to eat did not look edible. This was the worst food I ever saw! The eggs were green and the bacon didn't look cooked. The Drill Instructor said, "Sit down and eat." I was hungry. I put my egg and bacon in the grits. I was going to taste Marine Corps food for the first time. It was not grits! It was Farina! I Didn't like Farina. The Drill Instructor made me enjoy it.

The Drill Instructor walked us back to the Receiving Barracks. Before I knew it, we were in a classroom taking the ASVAB test again. Why were we taking it again? I just thought the Marine Corps wanted to make sure we were not a bunch of dumbasses. That day we signed a lot of papers. Later that day, the Drill Instructor started teaching us Drill. I am glad my family and friends did not see me. Educated men were acting like blooming idiots! We were taught right face, left face, about face, the position of attention, dress right dress, and parade rest. I did not know how vital count-off was. We probably did it a thousand times before our Drill Instructors picked us up.

Now about November 10th, the birthday of the Marine Corps. I arrived on Parris Island after 2400 hours, which was the 10th of November. That day we received a steak for our lunch. The Receiving Drill Instructor gave us more time to eat. We were told that it was the Marine Corps' birthday. We were not Marines and it did not mean anything to us.

We learned how to speak to a Drill Instructor. Things like, "the Recruit requests to make a head call, Sir. The Recruit is reporting as ordered, Sir." We learned port and starboard, which are left and right. It was around 1600 hours and the Receiving Drill Instructor had us outside for evening chow. Back at the barracks, the Drill Instructor has us clean the barracks. Before we knew it, we were taking showers. After showers we worked on a station- ary drill. The Drill Instructor did his hygiene inspection. Then he put us in our racks. This was how Platoon 1027 enjoyed the Marine Corps' Birthday.

Before we knew it, we were up and on our way to chow. After chow, we returned to the barracks. I was telling myself this was not going to be that bad. The first thing we did was make a head call (bathroom). After making the head call, the Drill Instructor had us pack our sea bags. It was 1000 November the 11th and the Receiving Drill Instructor had us outside in formation. What in the hell was happening? There were three Drill Instructors in front of us. "I am your Senior Drill Instructor (SDI), Staff Sergeant Lot. My two Drill Instructors are Sgt. Smith and Sgt. Hobbs. Welcome to Parris Island, where everything happens." Drill Instructors were in our faces. Where in the hell did they come from?

They were out of their minds, or maybe we were. The Senior Drill Instructor SSgt Lot told us to pick up our sea bags. "Put them on your right shoulder. You are too slow. I said drop them!" This went on forever. We had them on our right shoulder waiting to drop them. Drill Instructor Sgt. Hobbs, we could not understand him. But we did understand that push-ups began. What in the hell had I gotten myself into? The sand fleas and Drill Instructors were crazy as hell!

Senior drill instructor SSgt. Lot gave us a forward march. We were off going somewhere. The Drill Instructors got very crazy. I could not believe the pace at which we were going. Recruits were everywhere, including me. Sea bags were being dropped everywhere and recruits were trying to recover them. They wore our asses out! It seemed like we walked for an hour. This is well known as the sea bag drag.

Finally, the Drill Instructors had us back into formation. Lot stopped us in front of a barrack. Sgt. Hobbs put the platoon in two squads. DI Sgt. Hobbs had the starboard squad go first. The Drill Instructors had half the platoon on the starboard and half on port side. SDI SSgt. Lot and DI Sgt. Smith were waiting for the platoon. SDI SSgt. Lot was on the starboard side and DI Sgt. Smith was on port side.

DI Sgt. Smith yelled, "Portside face to the right! What in the hell did I see? Portside get your dumb asses back! Portside face to the damn left! Starboard side face to the right! How many rights do you have?" We were ordered to put our sea bag beside our right leg. SDI SSgt. Lot ordered star- board side to face to the left and portside to face to the right.

DIs were waiting for the platoon downstairs. "Platoon 1027, when you are told to fall outside, we will always start with the starboard side. Then portside will follow." "Platoon 1027, fall outside in formation!" "Sir, fall outside information. Aye Sir!" "Faster! "Faster! You are too damn slow! Platoon 1027 you will pay for being too slow!"

Platoon 1027 was finally in formation. DI Sgt. Hobbs ordered us to face to the right. How many rights are there? Madness was all around us. We were still in a state of shock. Finally, DI Sgt. Hobbs told us to start walking. DI Sgt. Hobbs, "Platoon 1027 stop! Recruits you are about as worthless as a boar with tits!" SDI SSgt. Lot told his DIS to locate themselves at different locations in the chow line. SDI SSgt. Lot sends in the fourth squad, third squad, second squad, and first squad. "Recruits, take a tray and sidestep through the chow line." We were at our tables; I do not know what we were eating. We were told to sit down. We were told to eat and keep our mouths shut. Some privates were confused. How do you eat with your mouth shut? All we heard was "eat." DIs were walking on the tables. Their shoes were in our chow, but we kept eating. Well, as fast as we went in, we left faster. We were so confused! Platoon 1027 was now back at the barracks. DI Sgt. Smith was teaching the procedures on how we would make a head call. "1027 you will repeat exactly what I say starting with Sir and ending with Sir. Portside make a head call," "Sir, portside make a head call, aye Sir!" "Starboard side stand by." "Sir, starboard side stand by, aye Sir!" "Portside clear the head!" "Sir, portside clear the head, aye Sir!" "Starboard side make a head call!" "Sir, starboard side make a head call, aye Sir!" "Starboard side clear the head!" Sir, Starboard side clear the head, aye sir!"

We were now back in front of our racks. SDI SSgt. Lot told us to empty our sea bag in front of us. "Recruits, you will receive a class in the morning on how to square away the locker. For now, place everything in the locker." We did as we were ordered. Some recruits were doing pushups and some- thing called bend and thrust. We would do many bends and thrusts before we finished training.

DI Sgt. Smith, "Tonight you will learn how to clean your body the right way." We were told to get all our facial hair off our face. We stripped down to our birthday suit. Then we wrapped a towel around our waist and we wore shower shoes. We were told to put our shaving bag in our right hand. We went into the head starboard first.

SDI SSgt. Lot stayed with the portside. We did not know what was happening exactly in the head, but it sounded like death! We heard DI Sgt. Smith say, "Clear the head, assholes!" Portside was on line and not look- ing all that great. Starboard side went into the head. Once in the head, the Drill Instructors put half of us in the shower and half in the sink room. The Recruits in the shower were told to wash their nasty asses. Most of the Recruits started washing their ass, not their face. Some of us got it right. The ass washers caught hell.

The recruits were told to change over—what a mess! We were running into each other! We were now in our new locations. DI Sgt. Hobbs told us to brush our fangs. DI Sgt. Hobbs said, "Recruits, shave your ugly faces. You will remove all the peach fuzz." One Recruit cut off his eyebrows. That night the sinks turned red with blood. We were told to clear the head.

All recruits were online. DI Sgt. Smith told us to put on a t-shirt and a pair of skivvies. We hung our wet towels on the back of our rack. DIs were still on the warpath. We had our bodies locked at the position of Attention. The DIs were up and down the line, checking our shaves and our bodies to see if they were clean.

The SDI SSgt. Lot had us get our letter-writing gear and double-time to the quarter deck. Then he told us to sit down, "Sir, Yes Sir!" "Recruits, you will write home and tell your family you are doing fine. You will give them your mailing address, which is your last name and initials:

Bravo Company Platoon 1027

First Battalion MCRD Parris Island South, Carolina 29 Now write ex- actly what I say. 'I am fine and have started my training. I have three Drill Instructors. I will be writing to you and informing you about my training.'

Put the letter inside the envelope, in the Top left corner, your address— middle of the envelope your parents' address. Then drop the damn letter in this box."

"Recruits, the two Recruits you see behind me, they are third-phase Recruits. They will take no shit from you. These Recruits are the fire watches for tonight. When the lights are out, they are in charge. Recruits, you will not get out of your racks until an hour after lights are out. Recruits get your butts online!" "Sir, aye Sir!" "Prepare to mount."" Sir, prepare to mount, aye, Sir!". "When I tell you to mount, you will attack your rack and lay at the position of Attention until the lights are out, mount!" The squad bay was so quiet. I was thinking, 'what have I gotten myself into?'

Before we knew it, sounds were coming from hell. The lights were flash- ing. The SDI SSgt. Lot was beating on a trash can. Recruits were slow to get out of their racks. The DIs gave a 'helping hand' to the Recruits that were still in their racks. We were online, I think. Moving around, we were baffled. DIs were in our faces; their breaths stank. Recruits were doing pushups and running in place. I was thinking, 'they are going to kill us!'

The SDI SSgt. Lot had us count off. There were 50 of us. "Portside make a head call!" "Sir, portside make a head call aye, Sir!" "Portside clear the head!" "Sir, Portside clear the head, Aye Sir!" "Starboard make a head call!" "Sir, starboard side make a head call, aye Sir!"

We were back online. The SDI SSgt. Lot had us get dressed. We did it as we were taught. Next, we made our racks; the DIs were all over us.

"Recruits, fall out for chow! "Sir, fall out for chow, aye Sir!" Platoon 1027 was now in formation. Dl Sgt. Smith had us face to the right. We were going to the mess hall. At the mess hall, the 3rd and 4th squads went in first, then 1st and 2nd squad. DIs were located in different areas in order to control us. We were rushed to our tables. We ate and we got the hell out. I had no idea what we had just eaten.

These were only a few hours that took place during November 1970. My three Drill Instructors, to this day, I will never forget their names. I have often thought of my Senior Drill Instructor. I was hoping one day I would see him again. That day came in 1982. I was a Gunnery Sergeant stationed at Parris Island at the Marine Corps Exchange. There stood a 1st Sergeant, my Senior Drill Instructor. Eleven years had passed. What was I going to say to him? Well, it just came out, "Sir, Gunnery Sergeant McNair Reporting as ordered." He looked at me and said, "Gunnery Sergeant." I stopped him and said, "Sir, I know you do not remember me. You were my Senior Drill Instructor. I was in Platoon 1027." Then he told me, "Senior Drill Instructor, I wish I did. That was a long time ago. But I see you have been very successful. I am in First Sergeant School, and I must leave and return to my studies."

It has been 39 years since I have seen him, but I will respect and love him like a brother. Thank you for helping me become the man I am today. It all started 50 years ago.

I retired as a Master Sergeant in September 1992. That same month I started teaching Marine Corps Junior ROTC. I taught for 21 years.

I am very proud to have worn the Marine Corps uniform for 42 years. Semper Fidelis. Once a Marine, Always a Marine.

STANDING AROUND FIRE IN A BARREL WARMING HANDS IN LATE DECEMBER

THIS IS ME WHEN WE WERE AT THE RIFLE RANGE.

I want to dedicate the first story to my Mother and Father. They are Carrol and Joyce McNair. They were great parents. They supported my deci-sion to go into the Marine Corps. My mother had to sign for me. Because I was 17 years old.

THE WORKING DRILL INSTRUCTOR

It is the 4th of April, 1977, a beautiful day in MCRD San Diego, California. It is graduation day for the new Drill Instructors. We have been in school since February 15. We have been trained well for this two-year tour of duty. My name is Staff Sergeant Larry McNair and I am graduating today. My wife Terri and our newborn son Larry Jr are here to see it. Graduation goes off like a charm. I am now officially a Marine Drill Instructor. After graduation, I took two weeks of leave. My wife and I were looking for an apartment. We found a very nice one. It was just what we needed.

It was time for me to report back to MCRD San Diego. I was assigned to the Third Battalion. Headquarters assigned me to Kilo

Company. I had to see Sergeant Major Lewis before being released to the Company. The Sergeant Major informed me of the dos and don'ts. We shook hands, and I was on my way to be a working Drill Instructor. The walk over to Kilo Company was one I would never forget. I was walking on the Drill Field, where many Recruits have been changed into Marines. I knew this would be a challenge for me. I told myself I would not let the future Marines down.

I walked into Kilo Company. My heart was beating very, very fast. The first Marine I saw was Chief Drill Instructor Gunnery Sergeant Moore. I was nervous and excited at the same time. We talked, and he impressed me very much. I was assigned to Series 3021.

Once I arrived at the Series, Series Gunnery Sergeant Bocook assigned me to a Platoon. He told me to pay close attention to what the Senior Drill Instructor had to say. He would be the one that trained me to become a working Drill Instructor. So, I would be working for SDI Staff Sergeant Brown. SDI SSgt Brown had a reputation of putting out good Marines. Series Gunnery Sergeant Bocook took me to meet SDI SSgt. Brown.

After the meeting, SDI SSgt. Brown put me to work immediately. SDI SSgt. Brown told me to introduce myself to the recruits. I went into the squad bay and gave my introduction. I was going all over the barracks, giv- ing recruits pushups. I had them get off their lazy butts. I had them pick up their footlockers and put them over their heads. The recruits were learning that I would not take any crap from them. Platoon 3021 was online at the position of attention. I went into the duty hut. SDI SSgt. Brown said, "I think the recruits do not like you, so finish what you have started." So I went back in the squad bay and continued training recruits. I had them repeat their general orders. I had the recruits do stationary drill movements. Right face, left face, about-face, and parade rest.

It was time for chow. SDI SSgt. Brown had the Recruits fall out in for- mation. SDI SSgt. Brown told me to take charge. This would be my first time marching recruits. Was I ready? I drilled the recruits like a seasoned DI. Once at the mess hall, SDI SSgt. Brown had the platoon form for chow. The recruits went into the mess hall like a well-oiled machine. The recruits were in their second phase of training. SDI SSgt. Brown said nothing. The recruits knew what to do. I was very impressed. Before I knew it, the recruits were outside, ready to go.

The workdays were long. I was on duty from lights on until lights off. I remember SDI SSgt. Brown let me leave early one day. That is, if 1700 is early. When I got home, I kissed my wife and son. My lovely wife Terri had supper ready. After eating, I relaxed in my recliner. Now I do not remem- ber this. Terri told me she tried to wake me up. This is how it went down. "Larry get up and go to bed." She had to ask me several times. Terri said I would not go to bed until I knew there were sixty recruits and sixty rifles on deck. Terri said, "Sir, there are sixty recruits and 60 rifles accounted for." So, according to Terri, I got up and went straight to bed.

The following day I was back training recruits. The recruits were up at 0500. They made a head call. I started with the port side, then starboard side. The recruits made their racks and then got dressed. It was time for chow. I got them outside in formation. SDI SSgt. Brown had already left for the mess hall.

Once Platoon 3021 was in formation, I gave the Recruits right face, forward march. We were on our way. Once at the mess hall, I gave them 'form for chow'. The recruits executed it well.

The recruits had finished eating and were outside, ready to go. I gave the platoon "Right face, forward march!" Once we were back at the bar-racks, Platoon 3021 held a morning clean-up. After the morning clean-up, it was time for physical training (PT). It went well. The recruits were very motivated. Back at the barracks, they took a quick shower.

The recruits had a morning class on first aid. SDI SSgt. Brown had me stay back. SDI SSgt. Brown wanted me to give Recruit Long some one- on-one special attention. "Recruit Long has been a pain in the ass for too long," he said. Without hesitation, I began training this recruit. Incentive training is the way DIs handle recruits with an attitude. I wore his ass out with pushups, run-in-place and bend and thrusts. Then out of the blue, Recruit Long stood up and said his soul had left his body! I told him to catch it and put it where it belonged: Back in his body. Recruit Long did act somewhat confused.

I informed the SDI SSgt. Brown; he told me not to stop. Well, I was surprised, but I did what SDI SSgt. Brown told me. The recruit kept say- ing, "My soul has left my body!" I was still giving Recruit Long push-ups. SDI SSgt. Brown came out of the duty hut and saw the recruit. Without hesitation, he called for a Corpsman. I thought the recruit was a blooming idiot! When the Corpsman arrived, the recruit got out of control. He was put into a straitjacket. SDI SSgt. Brown left with the Corpsman. SDI SSgt. Brown returned, but I was not told how or where recruit Long was. Later I did see Recruit Long and he had pulled a good one on me and SDI SSgt. Brown. Recruit Long was going home.

Before Platoon 3021 graduated, I found myself in a situation with the Series Commander, Series Commander Lieutenant Gray. I said something that pissed him off. To this day, I have no idea what it was. I was relieved by the Series Commander Lieutenant Gray. That same day I was assigned to the Sister Series. I was upset with myself. Had I hurt my career as a DI? I told myself only time would tell.

I met the new Series Commander, Lieutenant White. Lieutenant White told me not to cry over spilt milk. Lieutenant White welcomed me to a new start. I was beginning to think I would be okay. I reported to my new platoon. When I walked into the barracks, the Recruits did not call the barracks to attention. I immediately started giving them pushups. The barracks got very noisy. I wore their asses out. I kept them at the position of attention.

I walked into the duty hut and reported to the SDI SSgt. Hill. SDI SSgt. Hill said, "Who are you and what in the hell is happening in my squad bay?" I informed SDI SSgt Hill I was SSgt Larry McNair and I had been assigned to his platoon. I corrected the platoon for not calling the squad bay to attention. I could tell he was not happy. Over in the corner was the Series Gunnery Sergeant McNeil. He was the one who welcomed me aboard. Then all of a sudden, SDI SSgt. Hill welcomed me. I asked SDI SSgt. Hill if I could continue to train recruits. He told me to carry on.

I did not waste any time letting the recruits know that I would not take any bullshit. SDI SSgt Hill had me fall the platoon out for chow. He was testing me. I marched the platoon over to the mess hall. Once there, I formed them for chow. The platoon had some problems with the move- ment. Recruits were in the mess hall and sitting down. Some recruits were having a conversation. SDI SSgt. Hill did not address them. Platoon 3044 ate and got back in formation. I told them there would be no talking at any time unless they were asked to speak. I said, "Recruits that were talk- ing during chow I have your names. I will take care of you when I find the time. Platoon 3044, forward, march! Left, right, left, right. Platoon, halt! Platoon, left face! When you receive the command to fall out, you will get online. Fall out!" "Sir Aye sir!"

It was my time to piss them off. I had the recruits take their blankets, sheets, and pillows and put them in a pile. I gave them five minutes to make their racks. Recruits were moving like a tornado trying to find their sheets! It was impossible. "Recruits, just grab a damn blanket, two sheets, and a pillow, move!"

The recruits were busy making their racks. I informed them that time was running out. "Stop! Recruits, you are out of time. Recruits put them back into a pile. Recruits you have five minutes. Why aren't you moving! Recruits, you are running out of time!" I gave them a little more time. I started counting down from 30 seconds to freeze.

SDI SSgt. Hill came out of the duty hut. He yelled, "Recruits, fall out- side in formation!" "Sir Aye Sir!" They were happy to see SDI SSgt. Hill. It was time for close order drill. I was excited to watch the Platoon Drill.

SDI SSgt. Hill was working them pretty hard. Platoon 3044 needed a lot of help. When 3044 returned to the barracks, they finally made their racks.

I became very close friends with the Series Gunnery Sergeant McNeil. Series GYSGT McNeil would advise me on certain things. We both lived close to each other. On the drive to work and home, we had some terrific conversations. GYSGT McNeil was an outstanding leader. This cycle of training, he was heaven-sent.

The training was moving on like a well-oiled machine. I enjoyed report- ing to work and accepting the challenge that came with being a DI. Every day, Platoon 3044 became more like a unit. I could see they were well on their way to become Marines.

Platoon 3044 was now in the third phase of their training. We never had enough time to get things done. We were preparing for the final, personal inspection. There were things that must happen to make this a success. Recruits must help each other. There were always things that others could do better, like spit-shining shoes. When the uniforms returned from the dry cleaners, they always needed some touch-up. When it came time to tie their ties, it was a challenge for them. Platoon 3044 became very good at tying their ties. Recruits must and did help each other.

When the recruits were in their racks at night, the fire watches would clean the barrels of their M16s. The fire watch would use a cleaning rod and small patches. Before the recruits got into their racks, they would pull the bolt back and lock it. Cleaning the rifle barrels would continue until the day of the Inspection.

SDI SSgt Hill had the recruits try on their uniforms several times before the Inspection. Each time they got better at it. Platoon 3044 showed their pride when they wore the Marine uniform.

Finally, the morning was here. Recruits used the buddy system to get dressed. They inspected each other not once but twice. DIs would double- check them. The SDI said, "Platoon 3044, fall outside for the inspection. "Sir Aye Sir" Series 3041, all four platoons were now in formation.

Battalion Commander Lieutenant Colonel Aas was the lead inspector. Officers from Kilo Company were his detailed inspectors. Battalion Commander Lieutenant Colonel Aas would see all four platoons. Officers from Kilo Company were standing by to inspect the recruits. The inspec- tion was stressful on the recruits. The officers would break the recruits' self- esteem, but would build it up before he left that recruit. It was a learning experience for the recruits.

After the Inspection, DI's were briefed by the Series Commander Lieutenant White. Not to be disrespectful, but it was always the same thing. "Your recruit's shoes need more work, and their ties were too loose, the rifles were dirty."

"Recruits," I said, "Back in the second phase, I caught some of you talking. You were having a good time. I told all of you when I could find the time, I would take care of you all. Recruits you know if you are guilty. Have you seen this book? Do I have to call your names out? Come to the quarter deck now!" "Sir, aye Sir!"

"Okay, this is not all of you. There are ten cadets in the quarter." I could not belie this. Ten more showed up! "Well for not being honest, push-ups begin, run in place, jumping jacks, bend and thrust stop! Hmm you thought I forgot. On your back, on your face. You are too damn slow! Push-ups begin, run in place. Stop! Recruits get away from "Sir Aye Sir!" If they knew the truth? I did not have their names, or anyone's name, in my book.

The Inspection was finally behind us. The platoon was preparing for Final Drill. Drill practices became very stressful. There were four pla- toons competing against each other. There would be only one king of the mountain. The morning of Final Drill, SDI SSgt. Hill had the recruits to himself. SDI SSgt. Hill was getting them pumped up. My self and the third DI just stayed in the duty hut.

SDI SSgt. Hill was waiting in the reviewing stand. The third DI and I were with the recruits. SDI SSgt. Hill took his position on the drill field. SDI SSgt. Hill gave the command to fall in. Before I knew it, the recruits were in formation. Platoon 3044 was waiting for this day. As soon as they fell in, SDI SSgt. Hill gave the command, "Fall Out!" What did I just see, wow! The platoon drilled outstanding for the SDI. When the order of how each platoon finished, platoon 3044 had placed second. Platoon 3044 was now on a natural high; so were the DIS.

The platoon was now preparing for graduation. Series 3041 was having their first practice. The recruits did as they were told. After practice, the recruits started checking out of MCRD. Platoon 3044 received their pay and now started a checking account with the Marine Credit Union. Platoon 3044 had to purchase plane tickets and pay for their platoon books. Recruits who purchased rings and the platoon pictures paid for them.

Series 3041 had our second graduation practice. After practice, the re- cruits went back to the barracks. Platoon 3044 was getting ready for their base liberty; at 1200 hours, their liberty started. Platoon 3044 had to be back at 1900 hours. SDI SSgt. Hill had his DIs walk around to keep our eyes on the recruits. We met many of their parents. It was a pleasure spend- ing time with them. At 1900 hours, the recruits were back.

Graduation day. These recruits had waited for it and dreamed about it. That morning, SDI SSgt. Hill gave his farewell speech. SDI SSgt. Hill marched them to the theater. Platoon 3044 looked like a million dollars! Platoon 3044 marched their asses off for their SDI. Finally, the recruits entered the theater in a single file and were told to sit down. Parents were introduced to the Marines that trained their sons.

The Series Commander gave the Command, "SDIs Dismiss your Marines." They heard the last command they would receive from their SDI SSgt. Hill: "Platoon 3044 DISMISSED!"

Finally, these Marines had achieved their goal. May God be with you, Semper Fidelis.

This is Sandra Santos. Sandra is a dear friend. I dedicate this story to her. Sandra thanks for all the help you provided while I was at Okkodo High School.

Platoon 3131

Today Platoon 3131 is being received by Senior Drill Instructor SSgt. McNair. The receiving barracks Drill Instructor is bringing the privates to their awaiting Drill Instructors. Once he leaves, out of the blue, three men appear. The privates' lives are about to change forever. Drill Instructors are stressing the privates out and giving them hell! Privates are yelling and try- ing to repeat what the Drill Instructors are saying. Drill Instructors are in their faces—finally, Senior Drill Instructor SSgt. McNair has slowed things down. He tells them all what he expects from them. "Training will not be easy," he says. "I know you want us to be as hard as we can. U.S. Marines are the best fighting force on this earth. I am looking at all of you now. I want to see all of you on graduation day." All of a sudden, hell broke out again.

SDI SSgt. McNair yelled, "Push-ups begin--up down up, run in place, pick your knees up higher! Stop! Get your asses online!" Privates are scream- ing. Once online, privates could not do anything right. They were doing push-ups, running in place, running from one end of the barracks to the other. The deck (floor) started looking like a pond. SDI SSgt. McNair got the privates to the quarter-deck. "Privates, you will now receive your class on how to make a Marine Corps rack. DI SSgt. Hernandez and DI Sgt. Hall will show you how." The privates received their class and got back online. They were ordered to get their two sheets, a wool blanket, and a pillowcase. "Privates, you have five minutes to make your rack using the buddy system and then get online." Privates were moving as though their lives depended on it. DI SSgt. Hernandez yelled at the top of his lungs, "Stop! Privates, you have run out of time! Take all that crap off and throw it in the middle of the squad bay!"

SDI SSgt. McNair gave the signal to get the privates outside for chow. He wanted two privates to stay back for fire watch. SDI SSgt. McNair showed the privates how to walk the fire watch. Portside went first, then starboard. DI Sgt. Hall was waiting outside for the privates. DI Sgt. Hall had them fall in. These privates were confused and had no self-esteem. The DI's wanted the privates this way. They were told to face to the right. What a cluster f###! Finally, they did, and DI SSgt. Hernandez said, "Walk."

Platoon 3131 was on its way to the mess hall. The SDI SSgt. McNair knew this would be the most important day of their training. DIs must think like one, and this must continue the entire training cycle. "Platoon 3131, Stop!" DI SSgt. Hernandez had the first squad stand in front of the second squad. The third squad was in front of the fourth squad. There were two squads now standing ass hole to belly hole. The second squad entered the mess hall first, and the first squad followed. "Privates, you will get a tray then sidestep down the chow line. You will look straight ahead and hold the tray in front of you." They had no idea what they were about to eat. DI Sgt. Hall was at the end of the chow line directing the privates to their tables. SDI SSgt. McNair was waiting at the tables. "Privates, you will wait until all tables are full. Then you will sit down." The privates had never eaten so fast! Platoon 3131 went quickly into the mess hall and left faster.

DI SSgt. Hernandez was waiting outside. He had them fall in and face to the right. DI SSgt Hernandez said, "Walk." Once at the barracks, he told them to stop. DI Sgt. Hernandez ," Privates, you will have seven minutes to make your racks and be back online." The privates were confused. They were looking for their bedding. That was impossible. DI SSgt. Hernandez yelled, "Stop! Privates, grab some damn bedding, move!" What a sight to be seen! The privates were going out of their minds! The privates were at their bunks and attempting to make them—finally, DI SSgt. Hernandez yelled, "Stop! Get online!" The privates were being taught teamwork. DI Sgt. Hall with DI SSgt. Hernandez showed them how to work as a team. The privates finally got it and made one rack at a time. They were made as the DIs taught them.

The DIs taught the privates how to speak to them. "The first word out of your mouth will be 'Sir', and the last word out of your mouth will be 'Sir'. Do you understand?" "Yes, Sir!" they shouted.

"We just said the first word would be 'Sir', and the last word 'Sir'. Run in place, push-ups, run in place, stop! Now, get outside for a close order drill!" Here it comes. The privates said, "Get outside!" And they were stopped before they messed it up more. Yes, they finally got it correct, but it came with a lot of push-ups. Privates were in formation but still moving.

SDI SSgt. McNair said, "Privates, you have asked for it all day. Platoon, right face! Forward, march! Left-right, left-right, left-right platoon, (pause) halt! Privates face to your right. You are standing in the Pit. You will learn very quickly to hate the Pit. Run in place faster, faster, pick your knees up higher! On your face, breathe! Take a deep breath. On your back, on your face, Stop! Privates, you are too d--n slow! You had better move like a tor- nado! Is that clear?" "Sir, yes Sir!"

"On your back, pick your legs off the deck 6 inches! Do not drop them; hold 10" Ease your legs 5", 3"- stop! Keep your legs straight, ease your legs to the deck. Get on your damn feet! Privates, this is your first time in the Pit. Why are you moving? Get on your back! Too slow on your feet. Get on your face, breathe! On your back, on your face, breathe! Get on your feet! Brush yourselves off, use the buddy system. We will not take that sand into the barracks! Platoon right face (1, 2). Platoon forward march (and step). Left, right, left, right, left. Platoon (pause) halt! Left, right, Platoon right face! (1, 2) When you receive the command to fall out, you will get online, Fallout!" DI SSgt. Hernandez and DI Sgt. Hall were waiting for the Privates.

DI Sgt. Hall said, "That's right, take your sweet-ass time. Move your butts! I thought you were to be at the position of Attention. Get your feet at a 45-degree angle, heels online and touching. Privates, you look like hell. Looks like a sand party. Did you enjoy yourselves?" "Sir, yes Sir" "Louder!" "Sir, yes, Sir!"

DI SSgt. Hernandez said, "Privates, you will get a towel, a face cloth and shower shoes, and get back online." "Sir Aye Sir!" "Quickly! Faster, faster! Get your asses online! When I say school circle, you will repeat it. School circle!" "Sir School circle, aye Sir!" Move to the quarter-deck, move! When I say sit, you will repeat it. You will move quickly and sit down. Adjust, you will sit up straight and put your hands on your knees. You will cover down and align to the right. Sit!" "Sir sit, aye Sir! Adjust!"

DI SSgt. Hernandez said, "Take your towel and fold it in half. Now take your name stamp and put your name at the bottom center on the towel. The open end will be towards the quarter deck. Now fold your face cloth the same way and put your name centered on the face cloth. Get online!" "Sir, get online, aye Sir!"

DI SSgt. Hernandez stated, "When I say move, place your displays on the top bar of your rack." "Sir, aye Sir!" "Move!" DI SSgt Hernandez went on, "Privates, get online!" "Sir, aye Sir!" The DIs inspected the Privates' displays. Then all of a sudden, towels and face cloths were everywhere! DIs were on the privates like stink on shit!

SDI SSgt. McNair yelled, "Privates freeze! Find your display and put it on your rack now! Move, get this simple task done. All day, I have watched your lazy asses move like a turtle!"

DI SSgt. Hernandez got the privates' outside in formation yelling, "Platoon 3131, get your asses outside!" "Sir, aye Sir!" "Privates, you are mov- ing too slow. Move your asses faster!" SDI SSgt. McNair told the privates, "You will learn several movements today. Kneel." "Sir, aye Sir!"

"Privates, you will learn right face, left face, parade rest, dress right dress, and forward march." The drill session ended and with some success. SDI SSgt. McNair marched the platoon to chow. "Platoon, forward (pause) march! Step! Left, right, left, right, left, right! Platoon, (pause) Halt! (1 - 2). Form for Chow March."

The Drill Instructors waited for the privates inside. The privates were now sidestepping down the chow line. DIs were at both ends of the chow line keeping the privates moving. SDI SSgt. McNair is waiting at the tables. DIs are making sure they eat and get the hell out. "Privates, you are through, get out!" Platoon 3131 is in formation. The platoon then marched back to the barracks. "Left, right, left, right, left, right, Platoon (pause) Halt! (1, 2) When you receive the command to fall out, you will get online. Fall out!" "Sir, aye Sir!" "Privates you are taking your lazy ass time move!" Once online, the Privates counted off. They received a head call. The privates received a class on how to set up their footlockers. The DIs were watching them like a hawk. Some Privates had to dump their lockers and start all over. Finally, that task was finished.

The privates were told to get their letter writing gear and to get online. SDI SSgt. McNair called for a school circle. The Privates repeated it, "Sir School circle, aye Sir!" They received the order to sit and then adjust. "Sir, aye Sir!" "Privates, you will write a letter home. In this letter, you will write what I tell you to write. 'I have made it to MCRD San Diego. I am in Platoon 3131. We have started our training. I am doing fine and will write more soon.'

Pvt. Smith Larry

Platoon 3131 Kilo Company Third Battalion

MCRD San Diego Cal. 92140

You will put your parent's address in the center of the envelope.

Your address will be the top left corner. Seal the envelope and put it in this box. Get online!"

"Sir, get online aye, Sir!"

The privates are online, and they receive some bad news from the SDI SSgt. McNair. "After your breakfast has settled in the morning, you will visit the Pit. I will now refer to the Pit as Wonderland. Do you know why?" "Sir no Sir." "Because when you enter it, you will wonder when you will get the hell out of it" "Sir, aye Sir." "Privates, take your uniform off. Now take your trousers and lay them on the bottom rack. Hold your trousers at the waist. Rotate the waist until the legs are side by side. The legs should look like one leg. Fold your legs twice towards the waist. Fold your waist over the legs. Take your blouse (shirt), button all buttons except the top two. Turn the blouse over and fold your sleeves like an x. Take the left side of your blouse and bring it to the middle of your blouse. Do the same with the right side. Fold the bottom of the blouse halfway up. Then fold the top part over the bottom. Now lay the blouse on top of your trousers. When you get dressed in the morning, all you have to do is slip it over your head. Any questions?" "Sir, no Sir!" "Get it done now! You have five minutes!" "Prepare for shower call." "Sir, prepare for shower call, aye Sir!"

"Put on your shower shoes. Get one towel, one face cloth, and your shav- ing bag. Wrap the towel around your waist. When you go into the head, the shaving bag will be in your right hand. Drill Instructors take your positions in the head. Privates, you will make sure you wash your nasty asses! There will be no facial hair on your face. Get all the baby fuzz off. Get your damn shower shoes on now!"

Portside made a shower call and Starboard side stood by. "Move! Starboard side, shine your boots and brass!" "Sir, aye Sir!" Portside is in the head. Half in the showers and the other half in the sink room. The DIs are staying on top of them. DI SSgt. Hernandez says, "Start washing your nasty asses! Freeze, assholes! Wash your face first, not your asses!"

SDI SSGT. McNair is yelling, "Shave your face; all facial hair will be gone!" The sink room looks like a war zone. The sinks are turning red. "Brush your fangs now! Use some Listerine now! Change over now. Privates are moving like a tornado. The DIs have to slow them down. "Portside, clear the head!"

"Sir, portside clear the head, aye Sir!" Starboard side has finished their shower call, and Portside shined their boots and brass. "Get online for your hygiene inspection." "Sir, aye Sir!" "When the DIs are facing you, hold out your hands so they can see them. Privates, you will do a 360 so the DIs can inspect your body." "Sir, aye Sir!"

The inspection is over. "Put your uniform on your footlocker, cover on top of your uniform. Your boots will go in front of your footlocker; move! Quickly, get online. Privates, you will now learn how to get in your racks. Prepare to mount; you will move to the head of your rack. Mount, you will attack your rack and lay at the position of Attention. Prepare to mount!" "Sir, prepare to mount aye, Sir!" "Mount!" "Sir, mount aye Sir!"

"When the lights are out, you can adjust and cover-up. Third Phase Privets will walk the fire watch tonight. Do not give them any bull crap, only one private out of the rack at a time for a head call." Lights are off in the barracks. They are playing the DIs' favorite game; shut up. The SDI will take the duty tonight. The DIs have their last meeting with the SDI. SDI says I will see you all at 0400. "Do not let up an inch. We must be the same every day. Do not do anything stupid." At 0445 The DIs are on deck and at 0500 lights are blinking on and off. DIs are yelling at the privates.

"Get out of those damn racks and get online!" Some privates need help; the DIs are happy to assist. The privates are in a state of confusion.

They are looking around and moving. DIs are on them like stink on shit! The SDI tells them to get back in their damn racks.

"That's right; ass holes, keep playing this silly game! What in the hell are you doing in those racks? Get your asses out and get online, move! Freeze your lazy bodies! Count off! What a cluster. But a miracle happens, and they get it right. "You will get dressed, first your socks, then your trousers and your blouse. Just pull the blouse over your head. Do you understand?" "Sir, Yes Sir!" "Portside make a head call!" "Sir, portside make a head call aye Sir!" "Starboard side make your racks!" "Sir, Starboard side make your racks aye Sir!" Portside is out, and starboard makes their head call. Portside made their racks.

These are the first few days of Marine Corps Basic training. It will cer- tainly not be easy for the privates. But the ones that make it through they will be called Marines. I want to dedicate this story to Dan Ellison and Thomas Conley. They are the only Platoon members that have found me. Once a Marine Always a Marine, Semper Fidelis

This is Dan Ellison and Thomas Conley. These two men were outstanding recruits. This story is dedicated to them.

PLATOON 3057

Senior Drill Instructor SSgt. Larry McNair is picking up platoon 3057 today. He has two Drill Instructors on his team. Senior drill Instructor will be called the SDI and the Drill Instructors will be DI's. They are ready to go to work and standing by in the duty hut. The receiving Drill Instructor has set the recruits on the quarter deck. They are sitting with their hands on their knees. Their backs are straight, and their eyes straight ahead.

When the Receiving Drill Instructor leaves, the team marches out. They halt and face them. SDI SSgt. McNair introduces himself and his two Drill Instructors. He gives the recruits the same speech all Senior Drill Instructors give their platoons. He told them he wants to see all eighty of them on graduation day. Their training would not be easy. "My two Drill Instructors only know one way to train you, and that is hard. Drill Instructors, train these recruits to the best of their ability."

The Drill Instructors are yelling, and portholes (windows) are shaking. "Get your ass online, move!" The recruits have begun moving like chickens with their heads cut off! This was going to be the worst day of their lives. Drill Instructors were throwing sea bags everywhere. Footlockers were being tossed into the middle of the squad bay. Drill Instructors kept bouncing from recruit to recruit. Recruits were running to the end of the squad bay and returning. You could smell the recruits.

When the recruits were picked up, they had on a new uniform. They smelled just like cash sales (clothing store). SDI SSgt. McNair called his Drill Instructors to the quarter deck. He told them they all had to make an everlasting moment for them and for the Drill Instructors to follow his lead. Then he picked a recruit out of the blue. Poor recruit! "Do you like me?" "Yes Sir!!" he answered. Wrong answer! "So, you are in love with me?" "No, Sir!" This went on for a few minutes. The look on the recruit's faces was unexplainable.

The recruits needed to make a head call (bathroom). DI SSgt. Hall was teaching them what to say. But time ran out for a couple of them. So, DI SSgt. Hall just got them in the head and out. Then he put them on the quarter deck. SDI SSgt. McNair could tell they were very, very stressed out, but he did not let up; he told them they looked like crap. They did not impress the SDI. He said he could find better men in a graveyard. One recruit looked at the SDI wrong, and push-ups began.

He told the two recruits who had accidents to stay back. He told DI SSgt. Hall to have the platoon fall outside. Platoon 3057 was on the road for chow. They looked like a tornado was on their ass. SDI SSgt. McNair had the two recruits change their uniforms. It was done in a flash, and they caught up with the platoon.

DI SSgt. Hall would take them to chow. There are eighty recruits in platoon 3057. It is forty inches from one recruit's back to another recruit's chest. The platoon distance from the front to the rear is two hundred sixty- six feet. This required an excellent command voice. The recruits were given the command right face. The recruits had no idea how to march, so they were told to walk.

Platoon 3057 was now at the chow hall. SDI SSgt. McNair had the first squad take one step forward, and one side step to the right. They were now in front of the second squad. The third squad took one step forward, and one sidestep to the right. They were now in front of the fourth squad. "Platoon," SDI SSgt. McNair explained, "this is form for chow. Now return to your places in the platoon. Move! Form for chow, March!" Then he told the DIs where to locate themselves. One at the beginning of the chow line, the other at the end of the chow line.

SDI SSgt McNair would be at the tables where the recruits were to sit. He instructed the recruits to remain standing until every seat at their table was full. The DIs made sure they were eating and not wasting time. The recruits had a short time to eat their meal. All they heard was, "Get out, out now!"

Platoon 3057 got back in formation. DI SSgt. Hall gave them the order, "Right (pause) face!" What a cluster! It looked like a brain on drugs. The recruits did it several times. They were finally on their way; eighty recruits, two hundred and sixty-six feet of them. DI SSgt. Hall gave the platoon halt and left face. The recruits were now in the barracks and online. SDI SSgt. McNair and his DIs were waiting on the recruits.

SDI SSgt. McNair had Drill Instructor SSgt. Duncan teach the recruits how to make a head call. "Recruits, if you want to make a head call, you will learn the procedure. I will give the command portside make a head call. You will repeat, 'Sir portside make a head call, aye Sir!" After saying Sir, you will go!" Portside, when you hear 'Portside clear the head', you will repeat it. Sir, portside clear the head aye, Sir!' Now starboard side, make a head call." "Sir, starboard side, make-ahead call aye, Sir!" "Starboard side, clear the head." "Sir, starboard side, clear the head, aye, Sir!" DIs are still stressing the recruits.

DI SSgt. Duncan had the recruits get their footlockers. "You are too damn slow! Put them back! Recruits, get your footlocker, move! Put them over your head now! Lock your arms at the elbow. Run in place. Pick your knees up, higher! Stop! Put them down! Too slow, pick them back up!" Recruits are sweating from asshole to belly hole. "Put them down and freeze!"

SDI SSgt. McNair gives the command, "Quarterdeck, move!" The re- cruits repeated the command. They were asshole to asshole. They were covered down and aligned to the right. "When I give you the command, you will quickly drop to the deck. You will not move until I give the com- mand to adjust. You will put your hand on your knees. Your backs will be straight, and you will not talk until you are told to and your eyes to the front. Adjust!" "Sir, adjust. Aye, Sir!" "Recruits, you will now receive your class on how to make a Marine Corps rack." SDI SSgt. McNair tells the recruits that DI SSgt. Hall and DI SSgt. Duncan will give the class.

DI SSgt. Duncan says, "Recruits, get your eyes on me. Recruits, you will use the buddy system. First, a bottom sheet is put on the mattress. Next, put the second sheet over the first sheet. You will make your rack as they do in a hospital—tuck the top and bottom of the sheet under the mattress. Next, lay the wool blanket over the sheets—tuck the bottom of the wool blanket under the mattress. At the head of the bed, fold back your wool blanket four inches. Then fold the top sheet over the folded wool blanket. It will also be four inches. At the bottom end of the wool blanket, grab the wool blanket where it drapes over the rack. Lay it on top of the rack. Then take the folded ends and tuck them under the mattress. Make sure the blanket is pulled tight. Next, go to the head of the rack and pull it tight. Make sure all wrinkles are gone. Next, put your pillow inside your pillowcase. Center the pillow on the mattress. Are there any questions?" "Sir, No Sir!" "Get on your feet!" "Sir, aye, Sir!" "You have seen the buddy system. You have ten minutes starting now; move!" Like a bat out of hell, the recruits left that fast. First, they got their bedding and laid it on the bottom rack. Then, recruits started making the top rack. Before they knew it, they were making the bottom rack. Recruits had ten minutes. They were online before the time ran out. DI SSgt. Hall and DI Sgt. Duncan checked every rack. They were not that impressed. SDI SSgt. McNair saved the recruits from some crap that was about to hit them square in the face. SDI SSgt. McNair told DI SSgt. Hall to get them to the quarter-deck (classroom).

"Recruits, when you receive the command classroom, move your asses. Classroom!" "Sir, classroom aye, Sir!" These recruits were not wasting any time. They were covered and aligned. "Sit!" "Sir, aye Sir!" They dropped to the deck. "Adjust! Hands on knees, straight back, eyes to the front!" SDI SSgt. McNair informed them this class was on how to square away their footlocker. DI SSgt. Hall had a recruit get his footlocker and sea bag. Recruits were told precisely how to arrange the lockers. They were told to get online, "Sir, get an online aye, Sir!"

"Empty your sea bags in front of you. Put all your uniforms and other belongings in your locker, as you were told. You have ten minutes." DIs were walking around checking on them, having some of the recruits empty lockers and start over. SDI SSgt. McNair said to the recruits, "Freeze!" "Sir, freeze aye, Sir!" "Recruits, whatever the DIs taught you, it seems not important to you at this time. This is not just making a rack. It is being obedient to orders. Anything and everything taught to you during boot camp will save your life someday. The United States could be fighting a war at this time. Marines at any moment could be in combat and thinking about the Marine to their right and left. You are likely to be one of those Marines one day. Listening to us and remembering all that is said and done here will likely save your life.

Get those damn footlockers squared away now! DIs stay on their asses. Train them as if their lives depend on it! Teach them to respect each other! " "Get them outside for a close order drill." DI SSgt. Hall yelled, "Platoon outside for Drill!" "Sir, aye, Sir!"

SDI SSgt. McNair picked his platoon guide and squad leaders. "Recruits, who has had JROTC?" Hands go up. He had five recruits fall out of the platoon. He just started assigning them. "Recruit what is your name?" "Sir, Recruit Smith, Sir." "You will be the Platoon's guide. "And your name?" "Sir, Recruit Jones, Sir." "1st squad leader." "Your name?" "Sir, Recruit Hernandez Sir." "2nd squad leader, your name?" "Sir, Recruit Ward, Sir." "3rd squad leader, your name?" "Sir, Recruit McNeil, Sir." "4th squad leader." Drill Instructor SSgt. Hall placed them where they belong. "Platoon 3057, the first position I will teach you is Attention. Your heels will be online and touching—your feet at a 45-degree angle. Legs are straight, and hips square to the front, stomach slightly tucked in, chest slightly lifted. Your arms will be beside your legs. Your hands will be in a natural curl. Your thumbs along your trouser seam. Your mouth is shut. When I call you to Attention, you say 'Snap!' Platoon, Attention!" "Snap!" The Drill Instructors checked them. DIs were teaching the Recruits how important Drill is. The recruits did something. What a cluster! SDI SSgt. McNair went over Attention again and gave the command, "Platoon. Attention" Snap!" The DIs made corrections. The recruits were learning that drills would be a vital part of their training. SDI SSgt. McNair taught Dress Right Dress, Right Face, Left Face, parade rest, about face. He could tell this was a lot for one day but continued and had them sit down and watch the next command. "Recruits, the following command will be forward march. Now this one is very, very important. The preparatory command will be forward. It is informing you what you are about to do. The following command is the command of execution: March. I will use my Drill Instructors to demonstrate the movement. On the command of March! You will take a thirty-inch step with your left foot, 'Step'. Your right arm is six inches to the front fingers in a natural curl. Your arms are locked at the elbow. Your left arm is three inches to the rear fingers in a natural curl. Take a thirty-inch step with your right foot, 'STEP.' Your left arm is six inches to the front. Your right arm is three inches to the rear. Recruits, your arms continue to swing. Your hands are in a natural curl. Your fingers will brush against your trousers. My DIs will demonstrate forward March. They will march at 120 steps per minute. DIs, Forward, pause, march! Left-right, left-right, Swing your arms six to the front three to the rear. To the rear, March, DIs Halt. Fall out! DI SSgt. Hall will teach Platoon Halt. Recruits kneel down." "Sir, aye Sir!"

"Platoon- halt can be given as your either foot strikes the deck. I will teach it as your right foot strikes the deck. The preparatory command will be when your right foot strikes the deck. The command of execution as your right foot strikes the deck. I will execute the command quickly. Platoon forward, march! Left-right Platoon right foot, pause. Left, right--halt. You will take one more step with your left foot and bring your right foot along- side your left, right as in the position of attention." The platoon was taught Dress right Dress, Parade Rest, attention. Fall In, fall out, Forward March, Platoon Halt. The Drill session lasted one hour, and the recruits were ordered to fall out to the barracks.

The recruits were online. DI SSgt. Hall said, "Portside, make a head call." "Sir, portside, make a head call, aye Sir!" DI SGT. Duncan was wait- ing in the head. The recruits were running their mouths. DI Sgt. Duncan yelled, "Get your fat asses out, move!" Portside was back online. DI SSgt Hall said, "Starboard side made a head call." "Sir, starboard side, make a head call, aye Sir!" "Starboard side, clear the head!" "Sir, starboard side clear the head, aye Sir!"

SDI SSgt. McNair called his DIs to the quarter deck. "DIs, we have stayed on top of things, but the day is not over. I need a secretary and two recruits to keep our Duty Hut clean." DI Sgt. Duncan found a recruit with admin skills. He had the Recruit report to the SDI SSgt. McNair. But first DI Sgt. Duncan taught the recruit how to report. There is a knock on the SDI SSgt. McNair's hatch (door). "Who is pounding on my hatch?" "Sir Recruit Thorson Sir." "Why are you pounding on my hatch?" "Sir Recruit Thorson was sent by DI Sgt. Duncan." "Well, why?" "Sir, Recruit Thorson was sent to ask SDI SSgt McNair's permission to be the Platoon secretary, Sir!" "Get your ass in my office." SDI SSgt. McNair responded. "Do you know how to keep your mouth shut? Do you understand what you see or hear when you are in this office? Well, do you?" "Sir, yes, Sir!" SDI SSgt

McNair started teaching Recruit Thorson. SDI SSgt. McNair was impressed with his skills. Before Recruit Thorson left the duty hut, he had the 3 x 5 cards ready for the next day.

The recruits were double-checking their footlockers. They knew the DIs would be inspecting them after evening chow. SDI SSgt. McNair came into the center of the squad bay. "Recruits, we are leaving for chow—guide and squad leaders outside!" "Sir, aye Sir!" "Platoon 3057, fall outside for evening chow." "Sir, aye Sir!" The guide and Squad leaders were waiting for the Platoon. DI SSgt. Hall was watching them fall in. What a cluster! What a mess, all eighty of them! SDI SSgt. McNair centered himself on the Platoon. He gave the recruits, "Right, pause, face!" The recruits said, "1 - 2." This was their ditty to execute the movement. He said, "Forward, pause, March! Step!" SDI SSgt. McNair started calling a cadence. "Left-right, left-right, left-right." the cadence is very slow. "Swing your arms 6 inches to the front and 3 to the rear. Turn to the right. Platoon, pause, halt!" "1-2." SDI SSgt McNair has the first squad sidestep in front of the second squad. The fourth squad sidesteps in front of the third squad. This is called the form for chow. The DIs are located in different places in the mess hall. The recruits are sidestepping down the chow line. Finally, the recruits make it to their tables. The last recruit made it through and sat down.

DI SSgt. Hall is waiting for the recruits. He has them back at the squad bay and online. The recruits have made their head calls. "Open your foot- lockers," he instructs them. Every footlocker is taken to the center of the squad bay. DI Sgt. Duncan is assigned this class on how to square away (organize) their foot lockers. The recruits were sitting behind their lockers.

After the class, the recruits closed their lockers and put them back in front of their racks. The Platoon is ordered to prepare for shower call. "Sir, prepare for shower call, aye Sir!" They strip down to their birthday suits. Their uniform is folded and placed on top of their racks. Their boots are put in front of their footlocker. They put their shower shoes on. They wrap a towel around their waist, and they got online. "Starboard side, shower call!" "Sir starboard side shower call, aye Sir!" Drill Instructors are watch- ing them to ensure they clean their nasty bodies. "Clear the head!" "Sir; clear the head, aye Sir!" "Portside, shower call!" "Sir, portside shower call, aye Sir!" DIs are waiting for them. "Portside, clear the head!" "Sir, Portside clear the head, aye Sir!"

The recruits have on clean t-shirts and skivvies. The SDI SSgt McNair calls for a school circle, "Sir, school circle, aye Sir!" The recruits bring their writing gear and double-time to the quarter deck. "Ready, sit!" "Sir, sit, aye Sir!" "Recruits, you will write a short letter to your loved ones. You will say, 'I arrived at MCRD San Diego. I am in Platoon 3057. Training will last about 13 weeks. I am fine and will write again soon.' Fold it and put it in an envelope. On the top left corner of the envelope is your address. Which is:

Recruit Smith

Platoon 3057 India Company 3rd Battalion

MCRD San Diego Ca 92140. In the middle of the envelope, put your loved one's address. Drop your envelopes in this box.

Platoon 3057, get online!" "Sir, get online, aye Sir!" "Count off!" It went okay. There were 80 Privates on deck. "Recruits, prepare to mount." "Sir, aye Sir!" "Move to your racks, mount! Recruits, you will remain in the position of Attention until the lights go out. You will then receive the order to adjust." "Adjust!" That was the 1st Day.

At 0400 all Drill Instructors are on duty. SDI SSgt McNair has his morning meeting. "Keep the pressure on them. Do not have a brain fart! Keep your minds on our mission and goals." At 0500, the lights come on. DIs are greeting the recruits a good morning. "Get your damn asses out of these racks! Ass holes get online!" Some recruits have a hard time getting up. Not for long. They now have the help of a DI. SDI SSgt McNair stepped up, "You are too damn slow. Get back in those damn racks, take your sweet ass time. What are you doing in those racks? Are you out of your mind? Get your lazy asses online, Freeze!"

It was a pleasure training these men. They took the Final Drill and performed well in all parts of their training. I am in contact with some of them that were in 3057. After 42 years, we are using Zoom to stay in touch. The first Sunday of each month, we are together again. I had to stop them from saying "Sir," although some still do. After all these years, they show me nothing but respect. It goes both ways. I think they are funny and just being Marines. They were seventeen, eighteen, nineteen years old. They were full of energy, and some of them were full of shit. Platoon 3057 will always be men of honor. I dedicate this Short Story to Platoon 3057 and the Seven Men who made the reunion. Their names are Retired Marine Chief Warrant Officer Cleve Arrington, Jim Stack, John McMahon, Eric Gilberg, Kevin Coombs, Mike McDonald, and Terry Kerr.

We are Gorillas. We are tough and rough. We live in trees and ditches.

When women are rare, we will …. A bear. We are mean sons of ……!

Platoon 3057 In The Eyes Of Recruit Jim Stack

This Short Story was wrote by Recruit Jim Stack. He was in platoon 3057 during July and September 1978.

This is how Jim saw recruit training.

Jim Stack shares his recruit experience of Platoon 3057

That same excited feeling that was a blend of anticipation and fear was back again. After the first screaming greeting at our arrival, the NCOs in charge of us had let up some. I think this was to get us to let our guard down so that our Drill Instructors would make an even stronger first impres- sion. A good group of Drill Instructors work together like an improve troop on steroids. They set upon us like four whirl- ing Tasmanian Devils. Within minutes they had managed to dress down each and every one of us individually. They went from recruit to recruit spewing an unbroken stream of hostile obscenities. After they had given us each a taste of what we had in store for the next three months, they zeroed in on a guy named Wilson. It seems that at some point he had decided that he had made a mistake and in an effort to get a psych discharge had told our receiving Sergeant that he was hearing voices. He was definitely hearing voices now. Our Drill Instructors had posted themselves at the four points of the compass around him and were giving Wilson the ultimate surround-sound DI experience. If he hadn't heard voices before, chances are he's still hearing them to- day. All the rest of us were very thankful to him for taking the pressure off of us. Soon after this they shipped him off to one of the "rehabilitation" platoons. There were several of these with varying purposes. They had fitness, or "fat- body" platoon for guys that exceeded the weight for height guidelines, or for guys that were not in good enough shape to keep up with the training. They had a medical platoon for recruits that were hurt during training or were too sick to train. Then they had a discipline platoon for those that had issues with being told what to do, or whack-jobs and guys that didn't play well with others. This last one was where they sent Wilson. Recruits were kept in these platoons until they were deemed ready to join a training platoon, or until they were discharged. The fat-body and discipline platoons did all the menial tasks around the base, picking up every small scrap of paper and raking the dirt. The medical pla- toon we would see on their way to and from the mess hall, marching along as best they could with their crutches and arm slings. The discipline platoon they tended to keep people in for quite a while, the longer to f… with them. About two weeks before we graduated we saw Wilson marching past, still in the discipline platoon. Rumor had it that the heavy- weight boxer Leon Spinks spent the better part of a year in the discipline platoon, until they turned his tendency to hit people he was displeased with into a boxing career.

The vetting process that turns out Drill Instructors is very thorough and turns out a very consistent product. Ours were no exception. Senior Drill Instructor Staff Sergeant McCarran was a tall lanky southerner from the Florida pan- handle. He had missed out on Nam by just a couple years. I think this missed opportunity to kill someone rankled him and he took it out on us. He had one of those steely stares that made you stand up straighter when he looked in your di- rection from 100' away. Staff Sergeant Pucci was his second in command. A brawny Italian from Brooklyn, he was soft spoken, for a Drill Instructor, but the rows of ribbons on his chest earned during tours of Nam, were more than enough to garner additional respect from us. Then there was Staff Sergeant Tasi, a brooding, intense man from somewhere in the Pacific Islands. He had the kind of physical presence where you knew if he was standing behind you because the hairs on the back of your neck would stand up. I found him the most interesting of our DI's.

Every night there were always two recruits awake and on duty at all times, they were known as the "Fire-watch" and were standard in every barracks in the Corps. One of their Duties was to go into the DI quarters and wake the duty DI in the morning. The first time that Staff Sergeant Tasi was on duty we were all woken by a blood-curdling scream and recruit Cutter running from the DI quarters. Cutter had gone in to wake Staff Sergeant Tasi and found him lay on the deck. Cutter bent down to check his pulse. At this point Tasi had leapt to his feet in one motion causing Cutter to practically shit himself. Apparently Staff Sergeant Tasi liked to stretch out his back like this in the morning; we came to dread pulling fire-watch duty on nights when he was the Duty Drill Instructor,

The junior Drill Instructor was Sgt. Grayson. He had that young, cocky, self-confidence, like Eddie Murphy's character Axel Foley from Beverly Hills Cop. He seemed to make it his personal mission to break me down and I really felt that he was proud of me when I didn't.

Now that we had our DIs we began our training days, eighty days, God willing, to graduation. We now began our serious training and classes. With several hours a day of close order drill, we began our transformation into acting as a single unit. Our classes were on more serious subjects, assembly and disassembly of our M-16, weapons and tactics, and first-aid covering such situations such as how to deal with a sucking chest wound or traumatic amputations.

The most notable change now that we were picked up by our DIs, came in the frequency and manner of our disci- pline. We were now subject to "Pit Calls". There were many areas around the depot that were bare and covered with a fine dust. Whenever someone committed an infraction that really pissed our DIs off, or we started to get lackadaisical in our training, we ended up "in the pit" several times a day.

Many times when a single person f…ed up, they would stand to the side at attention and watch while the rest of us were punished. This was supposed to teach us that a unit was only as strong as its weakest link and to get people to shape up through peer pressure. When there were a few perennial f…-ups who repeatedly caused the platoon to get disciplined it also caused a building resentment. Blanket parties were rare, but not unheard of, we never had that, our platoon was more supportive rather than punitive.

The classic pit call started with calisthenics, usually "bends and thrusts", Bends and thrusts, while sounding like something you would encounter in a porn film, were not as fun as they sounded. Starting in a standing position, you would place your hands on the ground on either side of your feet while simultaneously kicking your feet out behind you into the up position for pushups. You then immediately execute a pushup, returning to your feet as you push yourself into the up position. These were usually done until several of us were unable to lift ourselves off the ground. Sometimes we would do standard pushups; these were done on the DIs commands with perfect form in an exaggerated slow pace. We were to stop with our chests three inches off the ground, the pauses in the down position became longer and longer. As one by one we gave out and our chests hit the ground we finished by lying flat on our faces at attention in the powdery dust. The dust was about four inches deep and as fine as flour. As we lay on our faces it covered us to about our ears, we were not allowed to turn our heads to the side. All the while our Drill Instructors poured a steady stream of invectives at us. As we belted out "SIR YES SIR" and "SIR NO SIR" in response to our Drill Instructors, small puffs would rise from the sides of our heads like miniature dust devils escaping from our ears. Sometimes we would spend the rest of the day with dirt caked around our eyes and mouths and filling our ears. Our DIs said we could wear the pit dirt as a badge of shame so that all the other platoons could see what a bunch of f...-ups we were.

As we marched around the depot it was clear what stage of the training the different platoons were at. Our training was broken down into three phases. The first phase was at MCRD in San Diego, days were filled with classes, drill, and Physical Training or PT, and we also took our initial Physical Fitness Test or PFT. Second Phase was at Edson Range at Camp Pendleton where we received rifle instruc- tion and did our qualification, followed by a week of mess duty back at San Diego.

Third phase began with two weeks back at Camp Pendleton for our basic infantry training. Then we were back at MCRD for our final three weeks of intense drill in preparation for our final drill competition, practical exams and uniform fittings in preparation for graduation. Looking at it from the first day of training, eighty days looked like an insurmountable amount of time, looking back, reread- ing my letters home, it seems to have whizzed by. I wish I had savored it more, that feeling of being young, invincible.

The transformation made in a recruit from day one of training to graduation is the most pronounced change in as short a period of time that most of these men will ever make. As we first began to drill on the "Grinder" a paved area a third of a mile long and larger than ten football fields, we had trouble keeping in step and couldn't seem to agree on which direction was left and right. Our tendency to run into each other was exacerbated by the roar of jet engines taking off from San Diego airport's main runway which ran on the other side of the fence along one side of the Recruit Depot. Every five to ten minutes the DI's drill commands, which were uttered in a guttural snarl from deep in the chest, would be drowned out by the scream of a jet taking off. The first couple of weeks any semblance of order that we had started to gain would dissolve into chaos as we each began to respond to our own individual interpretation of what we thought the Drill Instructor had said. As we bumbled around, learning the basics of close order drill, stepping on our own and each other's feet, platoons in the final weeks of third stage would crisply march past eighty boots heels hitting the pavement as one. Their bloused camouflaged trousers and starched covers were a world away from out rumpled sateen's and soft covers. We were the last boot camp series to be issued the sateen uniforms at the beginning. The sateen utilities were the dull green uniforms which had been worn in one form or another since before WWII, the same utilities familiar to fans of the series Gomer Pyle USMC. During Vietnam the jungle camouflage utilities had taken over as the field utilities with sateen's being worn in the rear, now they were being phased in for everyday wear and the sateen's were on the way out. The third stage platoons would march past in their crisply pressed camo utilities, with their gleaming boots and starched cylindrical covers, and we would marvel at the confident aura surrounding them as they moved as if they were a single organism. With our Drill Instructors screaming at us for every misstep and dropped rifle, these platoons on the cusp of forever earning the title "Marine", seemed a whole new species that we only had the barest hope of ever evolving into.

I think that the DIs had the most fun during first stage. We were continually pushed to make the learning curve as steep as possible. Sometimes we would return to our barracks to find all of the bunks that had not been made to satisfac- tion torn apart and piled in a huge mound of mattresses bedding and frames. Other times all the footlockers that were left unlocked would be dumped together in the middle of the squad bay, all the locks joined together in a huge ball of interlocked hasps. We would be given five minutes to get everything shipshape, an impossible task made harder by the continuous screaming of four psychopaths in Smokey Hats. The only way it was possible at all was through work- ing frantically together fueled by our shared hatred of our Drill Instructors. It became "Us" against "Them". Every attempt to turn us against each other only brought us closer together. Any military unit is only as strong as its weakest member. If you have the inner resolve not to quit, you will find the inner strength to push yourself to become stronger. We pushed each other to become stronger; we helped and encouraged each other. But our greatest motivation was the drive from inside; we did not want to let our brothers down. It is this bond, forged through shared misery, which makes it possible for men to function in the midst of the horrors of combat. We were beginning our transformation.

Platoon 2097

Today was a special day. I am Senior Drill Instructor Staff Sergeant McNair, and I and my two Drill Instructors would be picking up Platoon 2097. We had prepared everything for the pickup. It was November 1981, and this platoon would graduate in January 1982. Drill Instructor Sergeant Owens, Drill Instructor Sergeant White, and I were in the duty hut. The receiving Drill Instructor had the privates sitting on the quarterdeck (classroom). We three marched out to introduce ourselves to the privates.

I said the Drill Instructor Creed and introduced my two Drill Instructors. Then the privates had never seen three men in such a state, destroying what-ever was in front of them. The introduction lasted for about fifteen minutes, maybe longer. Then Drill Instructor Sergeant Owens got them back to the quarterdeck. The class was all about setting up the squad bay. After the class was over, the privates were ordered to get online. All you could see were assholes in a state of "What the hell is going on?" I, the Senior Drill Instructor, told the privates what I expected of them: that training would not be easy. "The days will be long, and this is our winter at Parris Island. You want to be a marine? Prove it. The Senior Drill Instructor will now be SDI and the Drill Instructor DI."

DI Sergeant White ordered the privates to get their sheets, blankets, pillows, and pillowcases and get back online. "Privates, you will use the buddy system. You have ten minutes." The privates were moving too slow. "Privates, grab all your bedding and get online. All you damn privates, move to the middle of the squad bay. Privates, about-face! Privates, throw your bedding behind you. Privates, you have ten minutes to find your linen and make those racks move!" Privates were stressing out. Sweat was pouring off them. "Stop…stop!"

Then I came out of the duty hut. DI Sergeant Owens had the Privates fall out for chow. I looked at them. "And you want to be a marine? You lazy asses. The day has just begun and no end in sight. DI Sergeant Owens, get them to the mess hall. Privates, you do not deserve to eat any Marine Corps food."

Platoon 2097 arrived at the mess hall. The first squad took one step forward and one right sidestep in front of the second. Then the third squad took one step forward and one sidestep in front of the fourth squad. "We will form for chow like this from now on. DI Sergeant Owens and DI Sergeant White will locate themselves at the front and rear of the chow line." I was waiting at the tables where the privates would be sitting. I told them to sit down when a table is complete.

"When the last table sits down, you have ten minutes to eat. Privates, you are playing a silly game. DI Sergeant White is waiting for the privates outside. Unfortunately, the slow game will cause you problems."

Platoon 2097 was back at its barracks. The platoon was back online. DI Sergeant Owens told the privates, "You will now learn what to say to make a head call. The first word out of your mouth will be 'Sir,' and the last word will be 'Sir.' Port side, make a head call. Repeat it now." "Sir, port side make a head call, aye, Sir. "Port side, clear the head. Repeat it now." "Sir, port side clear the head, aye, Sir." The starboard side said it the same way.

DI Sergeant Owens said, "Privates, when I tell you to move, you will find your bedding in the middle of the squad bay. Find your bedding; then make your damn racks, move! You have ten minutes, 'Sir, aye, Sir". The privates tried to find their bedding; then they grabbed some. The racks were made. The privates were back online. "Privates, get your footlockers. Place your footlocker in front of you." "Sir, aye, Sir." "Now get your sea bag." "Sir, aye, Sir." "Dump it to the right of your footlocker." "Sir, aye, Sir."

They were taught how to set them up. DI Sergeant Owens stayed on top of them. DI Sergeant White and DI Sergeant Owens were constantly checking them. DI Sergeant White said, "You were told exactly how to put your gear into your footlocker. Grown men cannot follow simple instruc- tions. Freeze your asses! Privates, push-ups begin. Run in place, bend and thrust. Push-ups. Stop! Privates, get your footlocker squared away. Move! Privates, get your laundry bag, towel, and facecloth and get back online." "Sir, aye, sir." "School circle." "Sir, school circle, aye, sir."

DI Sergeant Owens said, "You will now learn to put your displays on your racks. Privates, take your towel and fold it in half. Place the towel at the end of the top rack as you are facing it. The open-in will be inboard. Do it now." "Sir, aye, Sir." "Your facecloth will be placed on top of the towel, folded the same way as the towel." "Sir, aye, Sir."

DI Sergeant White said, "Get online." "Sir, get online, Sir." "Starboard side, make a head call."

"Sir, starboard side, make a head call, Sir." "Starboard side, clear the head." "Sir, starboard side clear the head, aye, Sir." "Port side, make a head call." "Sir, port side make a head call, aye, Sir." "Port side, clear the head." "Sir, port side clear the head, aye, Sir."

Then I said, "DIs, have the privates fall out for close-order drill." DI Sergeant Owens said, "Fall outside for drill." "Sir, fall out for drill, aye, Sir."

Platoon 2097 was in formation. I told the privates, "Let the drill practice begin." The two Dis and I looked forward to teaching drill again. I said, "Privates, all commands have preparatory command. It tells you what to do. The command of execution is when you do it. Privates, I will first teach you the position of attention. All marine drills are executed from the position of attention. The position of attention has seven counts. One: Smartly bring your left heel against your right. Two: Your feet will be at a forty-five-degree angle. Three: Keep your legs straight but not bent at the knees. Four: Your hips and shoulder are level, and your chest is lifted. Five: Your arms hang naturally; thumps are along the trouser seams, palms facing inward toward your legs; fingers are joined in their natural curl. Six: Keep your head and body erect; look straight ahead; keep your mouth closed and your chin pulled in slightly. Seven: Stand still and do not talk. When I call you to attention, you will say, 'snap.' Platoon, attention!" "Snap."

"DIs, check them. Get back. Platoon, attention." "Snap." "DIs, check them. Your next movement will be the right-face." During this drill session, the privates were taught attention, right-face, left-face, about-face, parade rest, at ease, and forward march.

DI Sergeant Owens took the privates to the evening chow. "Platoon, right-face, one and two. Platoon, forward. Forward march, step. Left, right, left, right, left, right. Platoon, halt and step. Form for chow march."

The privates were at their tables and were eating. The privates ate and were in formation. "Platoon, right-face, one and two. Platoon, forward march. Step. Left, right, left, right. Platoon, halt, one and two. Privates, when you receive the command, fall out. You will get online and stand by to make a head call.'" "Sir, aye, Sir." "Port side, make a head call." "Sir, port side make a head call, aye, Sir." "Port side, clear the head." "Sir, port side, clear the head, aye, Sir." "Starboard side, make a head call." "Sir, starboard side, make a head call, aye, Sir." "Starboard side, clear the head." "Sir, star- board side, clear the head, aye-aye, Sir." "Privates, sit down in front of your footlocker; make sure they are squared away. Next, check your rack display, and finally, make sure your rack is tight." "Sir, aye, Sir."

The DIs and I inspected the privates. Hell was breaking out in the squad bay. I was upset and was emptying footlockers. The DIs were giving the privates push-ups. The DIs removed the bedding. The squad bay looked like a tornado had hit. I said, "Privates, get this squad bay squared away now!" "Sir, aye, Sir." "I cannot hear you." "Sir, aye, Sir." "Move!"

The privates were stressing out. Their bodies were sweating, making ponds on the deck.

I then shouted out, "Get this squad bay squared away." "Sir, aye, Sir." "I told you, privates, this would be a long day. I am distraught with you all." Finally, the squad bay was squared away. "Get your asses online." "Sir, get online, aye, Sir."

I said, "Privates, you will prepare for the shower call. The first thing you will do is strip down to your underclothing. Do it "Sir, aye, Sir." "Fold your uniform, starting with your trousers. Hold your trousers at the waist. Rotate the waist until the legs are sideways. The legs should look like one leg. Now lay them on your rack, and fold them twice toward the waist, starting with the legs. Fold your waist over the legs. Take your blouse. Button all buttons except the top two. Turn the blouse over, and fold your sleeves like an X. Take the left side of your blouse; bring it to the middle of the blouse. Do the same with the right side. Fold the bottom of the blouse halfway up. Then fold the top part over the bottom. Now lay the blouse on top of your trousers. Leave them on your rack for now. Do you have any questions?" "Sir, no, Sir." "Fold your uniform." "Sir, aye, Sir." "Privates, you have five min- utes. DIs, check them. Once you have this done, get online." "Sir, aye, Sir."

Then I told them, "Get your laundry bag, towel, facecloth and this is how you will prepare for showers until you graduate. During shower call, you will shave, brush your fangs, and wash your entire body head to toe. You will get that peach fuzz off your baby faces—no hair on your face ex- cept your eyelashes and eyebrows. When you wash, start at your head. Your asshole and the baby maker will be last. Do you understand?" "Sir, aye, Sir." "My DIs will be in the head. Port side, make a shower call." "Sir, port side make a shower call, aye, Sir."

DI Sergeant White is in the sink room. DI Sergeant Owens is in the shower room. Privates, get all that damn peach fuzz off your face. Privates, start from head to your toes. Your head, not the head of your baby maker. Wash your nasty body. Put some damn soap on your facecloth. Private, why are you not putting your face into the shower? You had better do it, or I will help you. Port side, clear the head." "Sir, port side clear the head, aye, Sir." "Starboard side, make a shower call." "Sir, Starboard side make a shower call, aye, Sir." "Start washing your dirty body. Head to toe. Privates, brush your fangs. Shave your face. Starboard side, clear the head." "Sir, starboard side clear the head, aye, Sir." DI Sergeant Owen had the privates online. "Starboard side, put on a clean set of underclothes. When you finish, get back online." "Sir, aye, Sir."

DI Sergeant Owens said, "Privates, you will fold your wet towels and facecloth the same way you did your rack display." "Sir, aye, Sir."

"Move! Privates, now put your dirty clothes in your laundry bag. Put it on the bottom rack bar. Top rack, starboard side. Bottom rack, port side. Move!"

The privates were back online now. "Get your letter-writing gear." "Sir, aye, Sir." "School circle." "Sir, school circle, aye, Sir." "Move! Ready, sit, adjust."

I said, "Privates, you will now write your letter home. You will write exactly to your loved one what I say: 'I am at Parris Island in Platoon 2097, Second Battalion. I have started my training, and I am fine; I will write more soon.' Fold it put it into an envelope, and seal it. Now you will write this address on the top left side: private, your name. Second line:

Platoon 2097, Fox Company. Third line: Second Battalion MCRD. Fourth line: Parris Island, South Carolina. Lower middle: Write your ad- dress. Privates, put the letters in this box. Guide, collect them. Get online." "Sir, get online, aye, Sir."

I then said, "Privates, you will now have your hygiene inspection. When a DI is in front of you, hold your hand out so we can inspect them. Your body, from head to toe, will be inspected. The hygiene inspection is over. Take your uniform off your rack; place it on your footlocker. Put your boots on the port side—toe to the front. Put your cover [hat] on top of your uni- form, the brim to the front."

You will learn how to mount your rack. When you hear 'Prepare to mount,' you will move to the head of your rack. Prepare to mount!" "Sir, prepare to mount, aye, Sir." "When you hear 'Mount,' you will lay on the rack at the position of attention. Mount!" "Sir, mount, aye, Sir." "When the lights go off, you can adjust. Move your bedding back and cover up. Privates, there are third-phase privates walking fire watch tonight. They will not take any crap from you. They will not let you make a head call until one hour has passed. Then only one private up at a time. After that, there will be no talking. Play my favorite game: shut up. Fire watch, lights out."

It had been a long day. We DIs were tired. There was paperwork before any of us could go home. I would take duty tonight. I would be the Senior Drill Instructor for the series. The barracks were very quiet. You could hear a pin drop.

It was 0400 in the morning. All DIs were on duty. I informed the DIs that I wanted a hard reveille. "Stay on them. Let them know we DIs mean business." At 0500, the lights came on. The barracks were under attack. I was turning the lights off and on. The privates were confused. What was happening? Some privates were still in their racks but not for long. DIs were taking their sheets off them and I was screaming, "Get online!"

Privates were looking around. They were not at the position of attention. I said, "Get your asses back in your racks. Move!" A state of confusion was running wild. "Get out of those damn racks. Get your asses online—lock yourselves at the position of attention." I then gave the command to count off.

"What a damn mess! Privates, get your asses under control." The pri- vates tried it again. "Count off." They finally got it right. I then gave the privates a head call.

DI Sergeant Owens had the privates get dressed and make their racks. Their racks were made, and the privates were back online. DI Sergeant White was waiting outside, and DI Sergeant Owens would be sending the privates down. "Get outside for chow." "Sir, get outside for chow, aye, Sir."

The privates were in formation. DI Sergeant Owens gave the command, "Dress, right dress, and ready front. Platoon, right-face, one, two. Forward march, and step. Left, right, left, right, left, right. Platoon, halt and step. Form for chow march."

The first few hours of Platoon 2097 were the most critical training time. This was the glue that held them together.

I had to pick the guide and squad leaders. I kept the same guide and squad leaders the entire training. This was something my DIs did not like. They liked to fire, and I would put them back. I needed to find a private with some admin experience. This private would keep the DIs on schedule. I asked the privates. Who was good with a pen but most of all would hear nothing and see nothing. Private Thorsen was from Jacksonville, Florida. Did I pick the perfect one?

I explained his job, and he was a fast learner. But there was something special about him. I had somewhat of a dirty mouth. This I did not learn from my mother. I was always using four-letter words around him. This made him very upset, but I did not know that. Now he was an older private. One day he was standing at my hatch (door). He was very nervous. He asked me if he could speak to me in private. I said (using a four-letter word), "Speak." He wanted me to shut the hatch. I said I could not do that. Then tears came from his eyes. I said, "Get the F--- in here." I asked what was wrong, and he said he needed the Senior Drill Instructor to listen and not speak. I thought to myself, "Where is this going?" Well, he started talking, and it was getting heavy. Here came the bomb. "Sir, I am an ordained minister."

My lips fell to the deck. It was the first time I was speechless. Well, he proceeded to tell me he could not take all the profanity from me. Still, I was just listening. Finally, I could take no more. I told him to get the F--- out of my office. The private moved like a tornado was on his ass.

Private First Class Thorsen graduated Platoon Honor Man. The com- pany commander submitted Private First Class Thorsen for an officer pro- gram. He went home on leave with orders to report back to Parris Island when he graduated. I saw him when he reported back. A Marine Private Frist Class was waiting for an answer on his officer package. One day he asked me if, after he sent for his daughter could she stay with Mrs. McNair and me. I said yes. He had such a beautiful daughter. He was denied a com- mission program. The college he attended was not an accredited college. Some thirty-eight years later, he found me on Facebook. We caught up on our past, and I found out he retired from the army as a lieutenant colonel. Private First Class Joey Thorsen told me if he ever received a commission, he would save his first set of second lieutenant bars for me. Platoon 2097 was the Series Honor Platoon. This platoon took final drill, pugil sticks, first phase testing, and Elliott's beach final test.

You marines were tight. The respect you had for each other will stay with you for a lifetime. You wanted to be marines. You reached that goal. Semper Fidelis. Once a marine, always a Marine.

First Sergeant James Moore F Company Second Battalion

It is October 1981. I have graduated from Drill Instructor School. I reported to Fox Company Second Battalion Recruit Training Regiment MCRD Parris Island, South Carolina. The Chief Drill Instructor assigned me to a platoon that was graduating in ten days, which went by quickly. But before the platoon graduated, First Sergeant Moore relieved the Chief Drill Instructor.

Well, my life changed forever. It was about to get exciting. Now I thought I would let First Sergeant Moore know I was on my second tour. I thought this would impress him. Wrong! I do not think he cared, and

I had already put several platoons through as a Senior Drill Instructor. I could tell it did not impress him. But anyway, I told him I was ready to be a Senior Drill Instructor. Again, that went in one ear and out the other. It was time for me to leave, and leave I did.

In contrast, walking back to the platoon, I thought, how stupid could I be? After the platoon graduated, I went on a break waiting for I don't know what. I did not want to be around the First Sergeant because I embarrassed myself professionally. The word got out that my first tour was in San Diego; try to put yourself in my shoes. Parris Island is the real Marine Corps boot camp. I was a Hollywood Drill Instructor.

Fox Company was having a meeting with First Sergeant Moore, the first one with our new First Sergeant. I was thinking during the meet- ing, 'is this man from Earth? Where did this man come from?' It was the most extended meeting I ever attended. It was a one-way conversation, of which there would be many over the next two years. After the meeting, the First Sergeant informed us when the next Series would be picking up their Platoons. He named the Series Commander and the Series Gunnery Sgt. He had called out three teams, and it was time for the fourth one.

I was observing the Drill Instructors that were left. There were two SSgts and a Sgt. I looked around and watched the Drill Instructors as he named the Senior Drill Instructor. When he called my name, my mouth opened wide. I was happy as a pig eating slop! A Hollywood-trained Drill Instructor was now a part of Fox Company.

There was an adjustment period for me. I enjoyed training platoon 2097, but I had the feeling I was being watched by the Series Commander. One morning he called me to his office. He said, "SSgt McNair, why are you thrashing Privates?" "Because they were not obeying orders. Sir, I was thrashing a private when you called for me," I replied. "SSgt McNair, you are breaking the SOP!" "Sir, what are you talking about?" I looked at the Series Gunny and said, "What is going on?" I asked the

Series Gunny if I could speak to him in private. He took me into the walkway between the barracks.

I said, "Gunny, I need to show you something." So, we walked over to my barracks, and the first Private I saw, I told him to begin, and he started doing bends and thrusts. The Gunny said, "I do not have time for this." I said, "Gunny, I am thrashing this private." Gunny laughed and said, "We are not used to hearing this." I said, "Tell the Series Commander I will be glad to show him what thrashing is all about."

My two DIs, I think they saw the First Sergeant concerning me. Other than that, everything was just peachy. The First Sergeant did not call me down to discuss anything with me about my two DI's. Yes, I was putting pressure on them. But my job was to train them to be DIs and listen instead of complaining. It was a struggle, but I will tell you know they were damn great drill Instructors.

The First Sergeant had called one of his one-way conversation meetings. They would drain me of all my energy. I would go home to my wife and tell her about this out-of-control First Sergeant. She was an excellent listener, but I do not think she believed what I was telling her.

But as time passed, I realized I had misjudged First Sergeant Moore. I began to notice he was only making us better Drill Instructors and men. Fox Company was well-known at this time. First Sergeant Moore was pre- paring some of his Drill Instructors for the Battalion Meritorious Board. All the Drill Instructors he sent were selected and promoted. SSgt. Tully to GYSGT. SSgt. Hall to GYSGT. SSgt. Featherson to GYSGT and SSgt. Karam to GYSGT, and the list goes on.

I had trained several platoons, and First Sergeant Moore was going on an assignment to Marine Corps Headquarters. I was picked by First Sergeant Moore to be the acting First Sergeant.

I was surprised that First Sergeant Moore picked me. I now had my big- gest challenge. I took this assignment very seriously. I did not want to upset the reputation of Fox Company. First Sergeant Moore introduced me to our company Commander. The Captain was strictly by the book. I sensed he did not trust Drill Instructors. First Sergeant Moore was an outstanding Marine in all leadership skills. His personality was something you could not copy.

I sensed the Captain feared First Sergeant Moore, whose job was to advise the Captain, and he did that very well. When First Sergeant Moore left for Marine Corps Headquarters, he told me to call if I needed him. I did call a few times, and I felt First Sergeant Moore did call the Captain. First Sergeant Moore would not have given me this position if he felt I could not handle it. Working under this Captain was not an easy assignment. I believe the Captain was jealous of First Sergeant Moore's leadership skills.

After First Sergeant Moore left, the Captain had many meetings with me. We had several conversations that were not pleasant. The Captain tried to put some fear in me during the meetings. He would talk negatively about Drill Instructors. He always wanted to know what the Drill Instructors were doing. I briefed him every day. Finally, I just told him to see for himself. After he toured the barracks, he called me to his office and said the Drill Instructors were incentive training the privates while the black flag was up.

I said, "Well, what is wrong with that?" That is not what the Captain wanted to hear. He continued to tell me about the Standard Operations Procedures (SOP). Now I am not an expert on the SOP. He stated there was to be no training whatsoever during a black flag. I looked at him, and he was waiting for me to say, you are right. I informed him that the black flag was for training outside. The barracks were below the temperature of a black flag.

He got very pissed. I said training must continue and incentive training, well, it is training. I put up with mess like this until First Sergeant Moore returned. My fitness report card was not that great. The

1stSgt told me later that the Captain wanted to relieve (fire) me. I was glad to get him behind me.

One thing that I remember was he was an officer, and I was to obey lawful orders. He was the Commanding Officer of Fox Company. I think he thought he knew more than the Trained Drill Instructor. This Captain, in my opinion, was not of the same quality as the Marine Drill Instructor. He should have listened more to his trained advisors.

First Sergeant Moore was back, and Fox Company was in good hands. I do not know if the Captain was happy with his return. The First Sergeant never let the Drill Instructors talk or even think about talking pessimisti- cally about our company Commander. I honestly cannot describe First Sergeant Moore. I do not want to try. Because no one except the Lord and his lovely wife can.

First, Sergeant Moore assigned me to a series as the Series Gunnery Sergeant. The Series Commander was Captain Smith. He was an outstand- ing officer. It was a pleasure to work with him. I never had to advise Senior Drill Instructors. Drill Instructors have unique personalities. We can be a little hard to handle. But we have one thing in common, and that is training Basic Marines. I have four Senior Drill Instructors. When I had a meeting, things could get a little heated. They did not like my meetings. They were not as long as First Sergeant Moore's. Sometimes I had to put my foot down.

Every Afternoon we had Physical Training (PT). Senior Drill Instructor SSgt Featherson would lead the privates for me if I needed him. Senior Drill Instructor SSgt Featherson is a stud. PT always went outstanding. The Drill Instructors lead by example.

One thing that First Sergeant Moore demanded was attention to detail. I heard him say it at every meeting. So, I followed his instructions. Every day I left notes telling the Senior Drill Instructors what I found. I had to call a meeting, and like First Sergeant Moore, it was a one-way conversation. The barracks looked like something in a war zone. The

Senior Drill Instructors had a training schedule for every day, and it was demanding. If they were late, God have mercy on our souls. First Sergeant Moore would find out, and the Senior Drill Instructors and I got a peace his of mind.

The longer I was around First Sergeant Moore, the more I wanted to know about him. What made him stand out? Why did I change my mind about him? Why did I want to be around him more? The only thing that comes to my mind is my respect for him. Now some people may not believe me when I say this, but, first Sergeant Moore demanded respect. But it went both ways; he also showed respect. His famous meetings, his loud voice, was nothing but his way of saying, I care about you.

The Series was preparing for graduation. The Drill Instructors and I were not looking forward to all the practices. The First Sergeant knew the drill manual. Sometimes I thought that he wrote it. We could not be lackadaisical at his practice. He would correct you in front of everybody. We all thought he was wrong, but we did not challenge him. Now, as the years have passed, I understand why. You cannot waste time, and if you do, it will not come back. He was teaching us time management.

It was Graduation day. It was a beautiful thing to see and it went like clockwork. It was October 1983 and my tour was over. These two years I will never forget. The men I worked with were a blessing. First, Sergeant Moore taught me so much. I am a better man because of him.

Fox Company has a reunion every two years. We see how much we have aged. We laugh about our lack of hair. One thing we all have in common at the reunion is Sergeant Major James Moore.

This story is dedicated to Sergeant Major Kim Tully, one of the out-standing Drill Instructors and leaders of Fox Company, who passed away in July 2021. May he Rest in Peace.

SERGEANT WRIGHT

It was 0400 and I was on my way to the rifle range. I was still exhausted and half asleep. I would have duty tonight, another boring night at the range. By the way, my name is SSgt. Jeffery Jones. I was am Senior Drill Instructor with Second BN, Fox Company, MCRD Parris Island. I had been making this ride for over one year. I kept my eyes on the road, which seemed to be getting smaller. Then all of a sudden, there was a drill instruc- tor walking on the side of the road. I pulled over and picked him up. He thanked me as he got in and shut the car door. He introduced himself to me, saying, "I am Drill Instructor Sgt. Wright."

We started talking, and I noticed something strange about him. His uniform was of a different era. I wanted to ask him about his uniform, but he said he would get off here. I pulled over and stopped, and he thanked me for the ride. As I pulled off and looked back in my rearview mirror, it was as if he had disappeared. I stopped my car and got out; where had he gone?

I got back into my car and continued to work. Once I arrived at the barracks, I started my typical day. The recruits were up and dressed. They made their head calls, and then they made their racks. I had DI Sgt. Smith fall them out for chow.

I marched them to chow and try to prepare them for their first day of shooting. Once the platoon arrived, I formed them for chow. The platoon had made it to their tables and was eating. My DIs and I also enjoyed breakfast. I got platoon 203 outside for the march over to the range. Once at the range, I turned the platoon over to the PMI. The platoon was on the 200-yard line. The first round down range would be at sunrise at 0600.

At precisely 0600, the first round left a rifle barrel. I expected many safety violations. The PMI wanted those recruits to spend extra time snap- ping in after the last round went downrange. Platoon 203 held a police call (clean up) in our area. My DIs took care of the recruits with shooting violations, wearing their asses out.

I took the platoon back to the barracks so the recruits could make a head call. After the head call, the recruits cleaned the barracks. It was about 1500, and the platoon was back with their PMI. The PMI checked the recruits' range book; he saw exactly where they were hitting their target.

At 1600, the platoon went back to the barracks and got dressed for PT. Series 201 was on the PT field, having an excellent PT session. After PT, I took the platoon back to the barracks. The recruits took a quick shower, and then I took them to chow. The platoon arrived back at the barracks at 1800. I called for a school circle, telling the recruits how important it was for them to qualify. I could see it in their eyes. They were concerned about this portion of the training. I had the platoon get online and told them to prepare for free time.

The platoon knew what they needed to do during their free time. Time went by very fast and I had the platoon prepare to mount. At last, they were playing my favorite game, shut up. I was finally to myself and just trying to relax. I started to think about my ride to work. Did it happen, or did I imagine things? I tried hard to get it off my mind. But I kept thinking about what I saw, and I convinced myself that it was real.

0330 Tuesday morning, I'm awake, and I am still at my desk. What is going on? I took a quick shower; the recruits would be up in thirty minutes. 0345, and my DIs are in; I will let them handle Reveille. I leave early for the chow hall, needing some time to think. While I am eating my breakfast, I can still see Sgt. Wright.

'Why me, Sgt. Wright?' I wondered. 'I cannot let you control my thoughts.' As I was returning to the barracks, an extraordinary thing hap- pened. I heard a cadence and recruits' heels hitting the pavement. I look to my left, and I see a figure of a man, but he is by himself. I still hear a platoon. All of a sudden I saw a guidon. No recruits, I hear heels, and I see a figure of a DI. It cannot be platoon 203.

I need to get myself together. I will join the platoon and keep my mind on the recruits. Platoon 203 is on the 200-yard line. The first relay is in the sitting position standing by to shoot. "You will have ten minutes—ready on the left, ready on the right. You can commence fire when you see your targets, Targets!" The shooting day comes to an end. Platoon 203 is on its way to chow. I am going home as well as one of my DI's. DI Sgt. Hill has duty tonight.

When I got home, I told my wife Terri what happened on my way to work yesterday. Terri had a facial expression that I could not explain. "Terri," I said, "This is real. I am going to find out more about Sgt. Wright."

After dinner, I drove to the Beaufort Library. I asked for old newspapers that had articles on DI's. I read many articles, and finally, there it was. Sgt. Wright died July 1, 1970, of a heart attack on the way to the rifle range. He was found deceased at 0400 that morning. Sgt. Wright had a platoon on the range, and he was a Senior Drill Instructor. According to the paper, he was well respected by his fellow DI's. Sgt. Wright was training Platoon

203. I now had different thoughts about Sgt. Wright. I left and went home. I told Terri what I had read about Sgt. Wright and we both agreed there was nothing weird or frightening about him.

DI Sgt. Hill had the duty and the Duty SDI called for a meeting. It was now 1830. Platoon 203 was studying their knowledge. The recruits called the barracks to attention. SDI Sgt. Wright gave the platoon carry on and the command to prepare for showers. The platoon took their showers and had free time. DI Sgt. Hill was back on deck. He was mad as hell!

"What are you doing? Why are you on free time?" The guide informed DI Sgt. Hill, that SDI Sgt. Wright put them on free time. "Who in the hell is SDI SGT Wright?" DI Sgt. Hill was so pissed he just put the recruits in their racks. DI. SGT Hill went into the duty hut to make sure all paperwork was done for the day. Then DI Sgt. Hill took a quick shower. He was get- ting ready to call it a night.

It is 0300, and DI Sgt. Hill is awakened. He opens his eyes, and he almost pisses in his skivvies! SDI SGT. Wright informs DI Sgt. Hill it is time to get up. DI Sgt. Hill is speechless!

At 0330, I came on deck. DI Sgt. Hill told me about his night. I looked at him and said, "I have met him. So, the recruits have met him. For now, let's keep this to ourselves. Don't let the recruits know anything about this." At 0400, the recruits are up. Things have gone like clockwork, and the platoon is on the way to the chow hall. Platoon 203 and the DIs are enjoying breakfast.

After chow, the platoon is on its way to the range; the recruits have been turned over to the PMI. The platoon had a good day at the range. The recruits shot very well. I thought we would have 100% of our recruits qualify. I did notice that the PMI that we had earlier was gone, so I asked the new PMI what happened to him, and his reply was he went on emer- gency leave. This new PMI seemed familiar, but I didn't know why. I told him to keep up the fine job.

The platoon was on its way to chow—my DI Sgt. Todd had the duty tonight. Sgt. Hill and I both went home for the day. At 1500, the PMI came to the barracks just to answer any questions the recruits may have. The PMI had the recruits sit down at the rear hatch. DI SGT Todd thought that was a little strange and thought the recruits were too relaxed. So, he went to visit the PMI class. The PMI saw him and approached him. "SGT. Todd, I do not need your help, and I would like for you to leave," he said. Well, Sgt. Todd went to the duty hut and caught up on some paperwork.

It was 1700, and it was time for evening chow. After chow, DI Sgt. Todd had the Recruits field day the barracks. He made sure they were working as a team. DI Sgt. Todd Went back to the duty hut for some quiet time. He heard the barracks called to attention. When he went on deck, there was no one there. But the recruits were still locked up. He thought how strange the barracks felt. DI Sgt. Todd told the recruits to carry on.

DI Sgt. Todd inspected the barracks and found it excellent and clean. Platoon 203 prepared for shower call. "Sir, Aye Sir!" Platoon 203 has taken their showers and is now on free time. "Platoon 203, get online!" "Sir, Aye Sir"!

"Tomorrow is Qualification day. You must qualify or get sent to another series. Sleep on it tonight and pray that you do. Prepare to mount!" "Sir, aye Sir!" "Mount!" Lights are out, and DI Sgt. Todd hears, "Good night, Sir." And then he hears, "Good night, platoon 203."

DI Sgt. Todd walks on deck and wonders what the hell is going on. The time on deck is 2030, and DI Sgt. Todd is still wondering what is happen- ing. 'Am I dreaming? Is this happening?' It is now 0300 Friday morning, Qualification day, and DI Sgt. Todd is getting ready for the big day. At 0330, I was on deck. I asked DI Sgt. Todd, "Have you met our new friend?" DI Sgt. Todd replied, "What do you mean?" "Well, the platoon and Sgt. Hill has met him." DI Sgt. Todd said, "Strange things happened all night. The barracks were called to attention, and no one was on deck. I heard a voice say 'Good night, Platoon 203." I looked over at DI Sgt. Hill and started laughing. "What is so funny?"

"It is nothing to worry about; it's SDI, SGT Wright." DI Sgt. Todd said, "Who is SDI Sgt. Wright?" "SDI Sgt. Wright died in July 1970 here at the range. He was the SDI of Platoon 203," I told him. "What the hell?" Exclaimed DI. SGT. Todd. I said," Have all the recruits form a school circle." "School Circle, Sir, aye Sir!" "Sit! Adjust!" "Sir, Aye Sir!"

"As you have no doubt seen, we have had a visitor, "I explained. "I know why SDI Sgt. Wright is here. Platoon 203 was his first platoon as a SDI. He never made it to graduation day. I do not think I have to explain it any further. We must keep this in the platoon only. Who would believe such a story? Keep it to ourselves." Platoon 203 took care of their morning duties and now were at chow. My DIs and I were enjoying our meal. Platoon 203 had that look on their faces that said, 'this is my day.'

The platoon is at the range and waiting for the first round to go down- range. The first relay is on the 200-yard line. The PMI said, "Recruits ready on the left, ready on the right! You can commence shooting when your targets appear. Well, SDI SSgt. Jones, this is where the rubber meets the road." Platoon 203 moved back to the 300-yard line. I asked the PMI what he thought, and he just smiled. Platoon 203 moved back to the 500-yard line. The first relay was on the firing line. "Recruits ready on the left, ready on the right! Recruits commence firing when the target appears."

Platoon 203 has completed firing and is policing the line. The PMI calls for platoon 203 to sit down. He is looking at the platoon books to see where they hit the target. The PMI says to me that things look good.

The range officer called me over to the sound booth. I reported in, "Sir, SDI SSgt. Jones is reporting as ordered, Sir!" "What did you say to your recruits this morning, and what did you feed them?" the range officer asked. "Sir, is there a problem?" "Problem, problem? Hell no!" The range officer looked into my eyes and said, "Congratulations! The lowest score in platoon 203 is 210 Sharpshooters." I was speechless! I went over to the PMI and said, "You know their scores don't you?" The PMI had a giant smile on his face.

Platoon 203 was again on their way to chow. We DI's and the platoon had a great lunch. We knew their scores, but the recruits did not. Platoon 203 arrived back at the barracks. The platoon took head calls, and we're back online. I had thought that the PMI would be at the barracks. I waited, but the PMI did not come.

"School circle!" "Sir, Aye Sir!" "Sit!" "Sir, Aye Sir!" "Adjust! Well, this week of shooting has come to an end. Recruits, you have worked hard. But I don't know how to give the news to you." The recruits looked worried, "Ok, the lowest score was 210. Platoon 203 made history today! Wow, great scores! Get up and shout!" The barracks were beginning to vibrate.

All the recruits were yelling, "SDI Sgt. Wright!" over and over. Then there he was in his sateen's. This uniform has not been worn by Marines for many years. SDI Sgt. Wright looked at platoon 203, and he joined the recruits in their shouting for joy. The sounds could be heard back at the main side. SDI Sgt. Wright asked me if he could stick around until Graduation Day. The platoon answered, "Yes, Sir!"

It is now the third phrase. The training is moving fast. Platoon 203 has broken many records. Platoon 203 was known in all three Battalions.

I have been promoted to meritorious Gunnery Sergeant. DIS Sgt. Hill and Todd also were promoted to Staff Sergeants meritoriously.

Graduation day finally happened. The series did their pass in review and SDI Sgt. Wright was upfront with me. The Series Commander gave the command to the SDIs to dismiss their Platoons. "Platoon 203 Dismissed!" "Sir, aye Sir". I did not give that command. SDI Sgt. Wright had finally closed the book on Platoon 203 and then disappeared as the new Marines and their families left the parade deck. Their memories of SDI Sgt. Wright faded away as if he never existed. PARRIS ISLAND SERIES 100

Parris Island Series 100

It is 1970 at MCRD Parris Island, South Carolina. It is the month of December. Platoons are much smaller than summer platoons. The men that start training during this time of the year are a little harder to train. But when they do catch on, you do not have to repeat instructions over and over.

The Series 100 is informing, waiting to meet their Drill Instructors. Platoon 100 and 101 are ready to be picked up. Platoons 102 and 103 are still waiting for their recruits to arrive. The Battalion Commander wants all four platoons to be received by their Drill Instructors the same day. Thus, platoons 100 and 101 will be a little ahead of the two other platoons. Now, Platoons 102 and 103 have arrived. The 100 series is ready to meet their Drill Instructors, and each platoon has 50 recruits. These recruits are from the east coast.

December 8th at 0800, the recruits' world that they have known will no longer exist. Instead, men with a different vocabulary have just changed their world. The recruits have never heard or seen men like this before. They are now in their faces. "So why the hell are you here? Get your feet at a 45-degree angle, heels online and touching. Shut your mouth!" Out of the blue, four men wearing black belts demand them to pick up their sea bags and put them on their right shoulder. "Ah shit, how many rights do you have? I said, put them on your right shoulder!"

All four platoons are doing push-up running in place. "On your face, on your back, Get on your damn feet. Platoon 100, pick up your sea bags—face to the right forward march. Stop! What are you doing? Just walk."

Platoons 101,102 and 103 are following 100. Recruits are everywhere. Sea bags are being dragged by the recruits. Recruits are sweating from head to asshole. Platoon 100 stops, push-ups begin. 101,102, and 103 passed them. Then it happens; all four platoons have stopped. They are running in place. Drill Instructors are throwing their sea bags everywhere. Hell has found its way on Parris Island.

Platoons are mixed together; the recruits cannot find their platoon. Finally, the black belts re-form the platoons. It could be there or not. All four Platoons step off. The pace is getting faster. Recruits are falling behind. Finally, the Series stops in front of a barracks. The black belts tell the Drill Instructors to check them and make sure they are in the right platoon. The Recruits look like shit and smell like it. The Drill Instructors find their platoons and wear their asses out.

Now the recruits must find their sea bags. Series 100 will be on the third deck. Platoon 100 will be in barracks A 101, B 102, C 103 and 104 D. The platoons are in their squad bays and online. The black belt tells the recruits to double-time to the quarter deck. Once they are there, they are told to sit down. The black belt tells the recruits who he is.

I am Senior Drill Instructor (SDI) SSgt, Jones. These two Drill Instructors work for me. Drill Instructor (DI) Sgt. Smith to my left. Drill Instructor (DI) Sgt. Moore to my right. Drill Instructors, assume your position behind the recruits. Recruits, you are in platoon 100. Tomorrow is training day one.

"So, the first word out of your mouth will be Sir, and the last will be Sir. Do you understand?" "Yes Sir." What the hell, are you deaf? Do you understand?" "Sir yes Sir." "So you all want to be a Marine. Do you have what it takes? Well, do you?" "Sir, yes Sir!" This will not be easy. It will be the hardest thing you have done. My Drill Instructors are not your friends. Our mission is to help you achieve your goal. You may think that we are wrong on some of our decisions, but only time will tell. If you all see my Drill Instructors or me quiet, you should too. When I tell you to get on your feet, you will repeat the order. Do you understand?" "Sir, yes Sir" "Platoon 100, get on your feet." "Sir get on your feet, Aye Sir". DI Sgt. Smith waits for the recruits outside. "DI Sgt. Moore's recruits get outside in formation." "Sir, get outside in formation, Aye Sir".

The recruits are outside and are having trouble falling in. "Stop! You assholes are dumb as a rock. Get into the squads that you belong in. You have ten seconds. You are too slow. Freeze!" SDI SSgt. Jones is getting pissed. "Recruits, you had better get your heads out of your asses. Face to the right, walk. I have seen animals on a farm more intelligent than you. Turn to the right cover down stop. When you step into this chow hall, you will only eat and will keep silent. You will eat everything on your tray. Do you understand?" "Sir Yes Sir!" "DIs, take your position in our Marine Corps Chow Hall. Recruits, start with the fourth squad and continue until all of you are in a single file. You will sidestep down the chow line. SDI SSgt. Jones is waiting at the tables. Recruits, when your table is complete, sit down, and eat."

The recruits are at their tables and eyes on their trays and eating. DIs are moving and stressing the recruits out. Recruits are eating everything on their trays. "Platoon 100 you are through, get outside and in formation. Face to the right. Walk, hold your heads up and eyes off the deck." The platoon stops, face to the right. "When you are in the squad bay, you will get online. Do you understand?" "Sir, yes Sir!" "Move your butts!"

Platoon 100 is online and in the position of attention. "Recruits, you will now learn how to make an ahead call. The DI will say Portside makes a head call. You will say "Sir, Portside make a head call, "Sir portside make a head call aye Sir" "Starboard side, read your Marine book. Study your general orders. "Sir, Aye Sir!" "Portside clear the head." "Sir, Portside clear the head, aye sir!" "Portside is back online, Starboard side make a head call." "Sir, Starboard side make a head call, aye Sir!" "Portside, read your Marine book and study your general orders." "Sir, Aye Sir!" "Starboard side, clear the head." "Sir, Starboard side clear the head, aye Sir!" "Starboard side is back online."

The SDI is telling his DIs to teach them how to make their racks. DI Sgt. Moore orders two recruits to bring a rack to the center of the squad bay. "Recruit, get your linen. Recruits sit down, get your asses up. What are you to say?" "Sir Aye Sir!" "Recruits, you have been taught how to make a Marine Corps Rack. Get on your feet." "Sir, Aye sir!" "Move your lazy asses. I said, move! You have ten minutes, and you are moving too slow." DIs Sgt. Moore and Sgt. Smith are watching closely"Stop! Stop! Get online!" "Sir, get online aye Sir!" Both DIs inspect the racks. Linen is going everywhere. The squad bay looks like a war zone. Recruits are online and confused as hell. Some recruits are running in place and doing push-ups. Lock your damn bodies up, pick up that linen and get online! DI Sgt. Smith, grabbed some linen. "You have ten minutes to make your rack, move!" Ten minutes have passed, and the recruits are online.

DI Sgt. Moore's recruits, get one towel, a face cloth, and your name kit, move. Bring me a footlocker and put it in the center of the squad bay. Recruits make a circle around me move! Platoon 100 set down." "Sir Aye Sir". "Recruits, now you will learn how to set up your rack display. Take your towel and place it on top of your footlocker. Fold it in half the long way; now, you will put some ink on the pad. Take the stamp and very carefully wipe the excess ink off the stamp. There should only be ink on the letters. Now, put your name on the towel at the bottom of the towel, make sure it is centered. Do the same thing to your face cloth. Recruits, go to your footlockers and get this done; move!" "Sir Aye Sir!"

The DIs check them closely. Shit, what a mess. Grown men cannot fol- low simple instructions. There are several that must turn their towel over and do it again. "Recruits, look at the top rack. You will put your towel on the top bar. Recruits, place your towel at the end of the bar— the open end towards the Quarter deck. Recruits get your footwear." "Sir Aye Sir)!" "You will put them under the rack. The first pair, your dress shoes, should be touching the leg of the rack. To the right of the dress shoes, one pair of your boots. To the left of your boots, put your shower shoes. Recruits do it now." "Sir Aye Sir." "Recruits, move to the center of the Squad bay."

Recruit, get me your footlocker. Now recruits, this is how your footlocker will be set up. Recruits, go back to your footlocker and do it move! "Sir Aye Sir!" Recruits are dumping their sea bags and starting to follow the direc- tions of DI Sgt. Smith. Some recruits are talking. It is pissing DI Sgt. Smith off. "Stop just Stop! Recruits, get your shit together, and play my favorite game, which is shut up! Recruits, get busy; you are running out of time."

It is 1900. Platoon 101 is gathering up its letter-writing gear. SDI SSgt. Long says, "School circle, Move!" "Sir, school circle, aye Sir!" "Recruits, you are going to write to your loved ones. This is what you will say and nothing else. I have arrived at Parris Island. Training will start on the morning of December 9th. I am swamped with many very challenging things. Love you. I will write more soon. Top left-hand corner, your name

Recruit Smith Bobby

Platoon 101 Alpha Company

1st Battalion MCRD Parris Island South, Carolina

29905-6420

Put your loved one's address center bottom. Now seal the letter and put them in this box. Get online." "Sir, get online aye, Sir."

DI Sgt. Gore teaches the recruits how to fold their uniform. "Now pick up your trousers. Make sure the fly is open. Lay your trousers on the bottom rack. The trousers' legs should be together. Grab the legs and fold them to the waist. Fold the legs back until they are even. Put the waist on top of the legs. This is how you always fold your trousers. Take your Blouse (Shirt) and lay it on the rack. Recruits, you will button all buttons except the top three. Turn the Blouse over, x your sleeves. Now fold the left side of the Blouse, then the right side. Take the bottom of the Blouse and bring it so it is even with the top of the Blouse. Turn over the blouse and place it on top of your trousers. In the morning when you are dressing, you will put your blouse on like a T-shirt. Put your cover (hat) and place it on top of your blouse. This will go on your footlocker when we are preparing to mount. Recruits, take off those dirty skivvies and socks, put them in your laundry bag. Now tie the laundry bag on the top bar facing the portholes (windows)."

SDI SSgt. Long says, "Recruits, get a towel, face cloth, and your shower shoes. Now get your shaving bag, wrap the towel around your waist and get online." "Sir Aye Sir". "Portside, put your shaving bag in your right hand.

DIs, take your position in the head. Portside, shower call." "Sir, portside shower call, Aye Sir". "Starboard side, get your boot shining gear and brass shining gear." "Sir Aye Sir". "Move! Set down and shine your gear." "Sir Aye Sir".

The DIs put half the Recruits in the shower room and the other half in the sink room. DI Sgt. Hewett says, "You will wash every part of your body. That stink will disappear, and you will smell like a human again. Recruits, put soap on your face cloth. Start with the top of your head and go downward. Your other head dumb asses! Recruit, put your face in the water, I said put your face in the water! Wash your bodies quickly and soon we will change over. Move to the sink room. Change over now, I said now!" "Sir Aye Sir!"

DI Sgt. Hewett instructs, "All the hair will come off your face except for your eyelashes and eyebrows. Put the shaving cream on, and make sure to put it on your neck. All the baby fuzz will go tonight. Tonight, you will start to look like a man." DI Sgt. Hewett looks at every recruit, and the sinks are changing color. "How many of you have not shaved?" Several hands go up that explain the blood. DI Sgt. Hewett has seen this before, and it never fails that a recruit has cut off his eyebrows. "Recruit, you are a dumb asshole." DI Sgt. Hewett is trying hard not to laugh. "Recruits, brush your fangs. Time is running out."

SDI SSgt. Long calls out, "Portside clear the head." "Sir, portside clear the head, aye Sir!" "Starboard side, shower call." "Sir, starboard side shower call, aye Sir!" "Portside, put your clean skivvies on and a t-shirt." "Sir Aye Sir" "Put the towel and face cloth on the top bar near the window. Get your boot and brass shined." The SDI is walking around and checking on the recruits, who are hard at work preparing for the next day.

SDI SSgt. Long says, "Starboard side, clear the head." "Sir, starboard side clear the head, aye Sir!" "Starboard side, get some clean skivvies and a t-shirt. Put them on your bodies. Hang your wet towel and face cloth on the top bar facing the porthole." "Sir Aye Sir" "Portside, put away your shining gear." "Sir Aye Sir" "Get online. Recruits, in the morning after chow you will take the initial PFT. Recruit, you must pass it, or you will be sent to the Physical Training Platoon. Today you could not keep up on a simple force march. This training is not meant to be easy. Recruits that did stay with the platoon should be all right. I have not been impressed by your performance today. The female recruits would have done you in. I expect much more from you, and I will get it one way or another. Tomorrow night you will have one hour of free time. It will be after your shower call. This is not a screw off time. It is your time to prepare for the next day. And yes, you can write your letters.

DIs, hold the hygiene inspection, check them closely." There were no problems found; they will live to train for another day.

DI SGT Gore teaches them to prepare to mount. "Recruits, first put your uniform on top of your footlocker. Next, place your boots in front of your footlocker. Do it:" "Sir Aye Sir" "You will get back online. Now we will count off to ensure all recruits are present. Starting with portside number one through twenty-five. Then starboard side number twenty-six through fifty. Count off! What a cluster a monkey can do what you can't. Count off one to twenty. F g stop! I will step in front of you and say your number.

Do you understand?" "Sir Aye Sir!" "You will repeat after me. One-one-two- two-three-three". He continues all the way to twenty five.

"Well, I have been in front of you all, do not screw up. Count off!" The recruits got it right. All are present. "I will say prepare to mount. You will move to your pillow end and remain at the position of attention. Do you understand?" "Sir Aye Sir" "Prepare to mount!" "Sir prepare to mount, aye Sir!" "Move! Get back. What is going on in your little pea of a brain? Move!" The recruits are standing in front of their pillows. "Mount, you will get into your bunk at the position of attention. Do you understand?" "Sir Aye Sir" "Mount!" The recruits are in their bunks. "Recruits will get under your blankets on the command adjust. Do you understand?" "Sir Aye Sir" "Adjust!" The lights are off, "Fire watches no recruit will get out of their racks for one hour after lights are out. All recruits are in their racks one hour before reveal. Reveille is at 0500." The SDI SSgt. Long is telling his DIs, "They are playing my favorite game, Shut up. DI's will be on deck at 0400. Things went well today."

It is 0400. SDI SSgt. Bailey's Platoon 102 is up and briefing his DI's. "Okay, DIs what we do today will determine how the recruits see us as Marine Drill Instructors. Be stern but fair, do not make a stupid mistake like your hands doing something they should not. Yesterday was a good day, but it is in the past."

At 0445, the Drill Instructors are on deck. At 0500 SDI, SSgt. Bailey turns on the lights. DIs are yelling, "Get out of those damn racks." The SDI SSgt. Bailey yells, "Get your ass up." Lights are going off and on. Di's are yelling, "Get online." Recruits are still in their racks, but not for long. DI Sgt. Russ is playing reach out and touch someone like AT&T. Once the recruits are out of their racks, they are being turned over. "Recruits, lock your damn bodies up." SDI SSgt. Bailey is very pissed at the recruits today. "I am taking you to Wonderland. And why is it called Wonderland? You will find out. Count off! One, two, three, four, five, all the way to fifty. Starboard side make a head call." "Sir, starboard side make a head call, aye Sir" "Clear the head! "Sir, starboard side clear the head, aye Sir". "Portside make a head call." "Sir, portside make a head call, aye Sir" "Clear the head!" "Sir portside clear the head aye Sir".

Platoon 102, get your trousers put them on. Adjust your belt and lock it. Next, pull your blouse over your head. Button the three top buttons. Sit down on your footlocker, put your socks on. Now put on your boots, lace them to the top and tuck the extra boot strings inside your boots. Now put your field jacket on the top of your footlocker. Recruits make your rack; you have five minutes. Recruits move, make these racks quickly. Recruits, put on your field Jacket, button, and zip them up. Platoon 102 get outside for chow. The chow hall is waiting on us. Face to the right, walk, stay covered down."

SDI SSgt. Bailey gives the platoon a halt. "DIs take your places in the chow hall. If it is on your tray, you will eat it." DIs are walking around the tables. "Recruits, sit up straight. Chew with your mouth shut.

Platoon 102 is outside and in in formation. Sgt. Walker marches the platoon back to the barracks. He has the platoon take everything off except their t-shirt. Break out your jock.

SDI SSgt Bailey tells his DIs to get the squad bay clean. DI Sgt. Russ takes the 3rd and 4th squad. They will learn to field day the head, quarter- deck, and stairwells. DI Sgt. Walker has 1st and 2nd squad. They will clean the squad bay. The DIs are showing the recruits what they must do.

DI Sgt. Walker says, "Recruits, get online." "Sir, get online, aye Sir". "Recruits, get your war belt and canteen." I SSgt. Bailey is speaking to them. "Okay, recruits, you will be taking the initial Physical Strength Test (PFT) this morning. You must pass this test—a minimum of 3 pull ups, 40 sit ups, and the one-and-a-half-mile run." The platoon is marching to the Pt field. Series 100 are all there.

The Series Commander Lt. Gore is speaking to them. "If you do not pass this test, you will be sent to the Physical Fitness Platoon. SDIs, All the platoons have staged their gear."

Platoons 100 and 101 have formed up at the pullup bars. Platoons 102 and 103 are standing by for their sit ups. The exercises have begun; weird sounds are coming from the Recruits. Platoons 100 and 101 have recruits who failed the pull-ups and sit ups. In platoon 102 and 103, all of the recruits passed the sit ups and pullups. The recruits are motivated and working hard.

The Series Commander Lt. Shore now explains the run and its route. "Recruits, you must finish the run in less than fourteen minutes. There will be DIs along the route to ensure you are going the right way. Again, you must beat fourteen minutes. You will start when the whistle blows."

The whistle has blown, and the recruits have begun. The SDIs are running with the Series. Recruits are stopping and are encouraged to continue. The recruits have finished the run. Some have been put in a truck because they could not finish. The Series will drop ten Recruits because they could not pass the test.

Series 100 is on the move back to the barracks. The Series is back at their barracks. The recruits will shower, and they will receive the M14 (rifle) today. Series 100 is now on its way to the Base Armory. Platoon 103 has lined up to enter the Armory. Recruits will step up to the Marine who is behind a wire gage. Each recruit will sign for their rifle, and then the Marine will give it to them. The SDI SSgt. Jones is watching his recruits sign for the rifle. Platoon 103 has their rifles, and they are back information. SDI SSgt. Hughes is teaching them how to hold the rifle. They are learning to hold the rifle beside their right leg. Next, SDI SSgt. Hughes will teach port arms. SDI SSgt. Hughes explains this is just the beginning of the rifle movements.

Platoon 102 SDI SSgt Bailey has promised them a trip to Wonderland. "Platoon halt, Forward march, platoon halt, about face. Run in place, bend and thrust, push-ups, on your face breath, smell Parris Island, breath on your back. Run in place, STOP! This is Wonderland. Now, why do I call it Wonderland? I will tell you because you are wondering when this will stop!"

Platoon 103 is back at the barracks. The platoon is online with their rifles. DI Sgt. Duncan has a rifle brought to the center of the squad bay. The recruits are sitting down to learn how to secure their rifles. The recruits have their rifle locks. "The barrel will face the deck (floor). You will put the lock and its wire cable through the firing mechanism. And then, you will make sure the lock is locked. Recruits, do not think you can cheat on unlocking your lock. Once you lock it, make sure you turn the lock several times. If you think you can outsmart us, think again. Portside, make a head call." "Sir, portside make a head call, aye Sir" "Portside, clear the head." "Sir, portside clear the head, aye Sir" "Starboard side, make a head call." "Sir,

Starboard side make a head call, aye Sir" "Starboard side, clear the head. ""Sir starboard side clear the head aye Sir".

SDI SSgt. Hewitt tells his DI to have the platoon fall out for drill. DI Sgt. Duncan is waiting for them downstairs. The platoon is having trouble falling in. "Freeze! What the hell is going on? Get your heads out of your asses."

DI Sgt. Duncan teaches Dress right Dress. "Recruits, your left arm is parallel to the deck, just touching the recruit's shoulder to your left. Your palm is flat, and your fingers are extended and joined. Your head is turned 45 degrees to the right. Recruits, you will sidestep to the right or left, take short choppy steps forward or backward, until you are aligned to the right. On the command ready front, you will drop your left arm and return your head to the front. This is done with precision and very fast. Your next com- mand is cover! You will move left or fight to cover on the recruit in front of you. Dress Right Dress. Recruits, you are too slow get back. Dress right Dress! You are too damn slow. Get your eyeballs on me, you will say snap. Your arms will come up a thousand miles per hour. Your head will turn 45 degrees to the right. Let us try this again. Dress right Dress! Snap! Ready front snap! Cover (1, 2, 3)!"

SDI SSgt. Hewitt is now with the recruits. "Recruits, we will pick up where you were after chow." The platoon has been to chow and made head calls. "Recruits, kneel down. I will now teach you to march. The command will be a forward march. All drills have preparatory command and the com- mand of execution. The preparatory command is telling you what you are about to do. Okay, like right, you know you are about to do something to the right. The command of execution is face! Forward (pause) march! You will take a thirty-inch step with your left foot. Your right arm will swing six inches to the front, and your fingers will be in a natural curl. Your left arm will swing three inches to the rear, fingers in a natural curl. Your arms will be locked at the elbow. Your fingers will brush against your legs. You will take a thirty-inch step with your right foot. You will continue this motion until you receive platoon halt. Recruits' platoon halt may be given as your right, or left foot strikes the deck. I will teach it as your right foot strikes the deck. Take a step with your right foot. Platoon, take a step with your left foot (pause) take a step with your right foot halt! When you hear halt, you will take one more step with your left foot and bring your right foot against your left. Step with your right foot you will hear halt. Take one more step with your left foot. Bring your right foot alongside your left foot. Your heels will be online and touching. Platoon 103, let us try it. Platoon, when you hear Forward March, you will say step. "Sir aye Sir!" "Forward (pause) march! (Step) left, right, left, right, left, right. Platoon (pause) right halt (left-right, freeze)."

Platoon 103 is on their way to evening chow. SDI SSgt Hewitt is march- ing them. "Left, right, left, right, left, right, left, right. Platoon (pause) halt (left-right) Freeze!" The third squad will take one step forward, and then one sidestep to your right. The first squad takes one step forward, and the one sidesteps to your right. Recruits, this is how we will form for chow. Do you understand? "Sir, yes Sir!" The platoon is now entering the chow hall, getting their trays, and sidestepping down the chow line. The SDI is waiting at their tables. "Platoon 103, let's eat and get the hell out."

Platoons 100,101 and 102 are also eating at this time. The SDIs are discussing what has happened during the PFT. The Series Commander has informed them they have dropped twenty recruits as a series but to stand by for the pick-ups to start arriving.

The platoons have left the mess hall. The Series Commander informed the SDIs to give the class on the M14 rifle. The platoons are back in their squad bays and receiving the class on the M14. They have learned to take it apart and to resemble the rifle. The Recruits are securing their rifles to their racks.

DIs check the rifle to ensure they are secure. DI finds one rifle not secured. He takes the rifle and the Recruit to the middle of the squad bay.

DI tells the platoon how easy it is to lose your rifle. If this were a combat situation and the Marine lost his rifle, he would endanger his fellow Marines. Without a rifle, a Marine is not worth a crap. Push-ups begin doing them until I am tired. This recruit is not paying attention to detail. Who told you to stop? Run in place, bend and thrust, push-ups, Stop! Lock this rifle to your rack now!"

All platoons are preparing to make shower calls. The Series has finished their shower call. And are in free time. This is the time they have to write letters and prepare for the next day. They have one hour. After that hour has passed, Recruits are online for their hygiene inspection. The platoons have blisters on their feet. The DIs inform them they will give them moleskin in the morning. This will make it easier to wear boots.

SDI SSgt. Jones tells platoon 100 to prepare to mount. They are standing in front of their pillows. "Mount, adjust, play my favorite game, shut up."

This Series will continue to train. This is the first phase. They have the 2nd and 3rd phases to Complete. This is not the end.

THE DAY OF THE STORM

It is August 1, 2021; Parris Island is busy training recruits. The recruits may get a morning PT and a class in before the black flag goes up. The flag conditions are green, yellow, red, and black—the dreaded black flag. The temperature during a green is 80-84.9, yellow 85-87.9, red 88-89.9, and black, 90 and above. DIs are constantly checking what flag is flying. The flags are in front of each company, parade deck, chow hall, PT field, Battalion Headquarters, and Regimental Headquarters.

Parris Island is located just out of the Beaufort city limits. During August and September, Parris Island is very aware of hurricanes. It has an evacu-ation plan. That plan takes the recruits to Marine Corps Base,

Albany, Georgia. 1st Battalion is near the waterway. Bravo Company has three series on deck, series 104, series 108, and series 112. Bravo Company has 900 recruits in training and 12 DIs in each series, plus one Lieutenant and Gunnery Sergeant.

It is August 2, and the National Weather Service is tracking a tropical depression (Tammy) in the Atlantic. It has winds gusting 40 miles per hour moving northwest. Training is continuing, and the storm is still blowing in the Atlantic. Series 104 is on the PT field. Series 108 and 112 are just arriving for their morning PT session. The series commanders know that the green flag is flying. The PT session went well. The recruits are back at the barracks. The DIs have the recruits online, ready to take a quick shower. All three series have their showers and are dressed. The DIs have the recruits hold a morning clean-up. After morning clean-up, the day continues.

Series 104 has a first aid class, series 108 has drill, and series 112 has a rifle class. It is 0900 and the yellow flag is flying. It is 85 degrees and climb- ing. Series 108 must pay close attention to the flag and the temperature. We have a red flag on Parris Island. The drill has ended, and 108 series are returning to their barracks. Series 104 has returned and is online. All three series are in their barracks and will continue cleaning their barracks until time to go to lunch.

"Platoon 104 get online!" "Sir, get online aye Sir!" "Guide and squad leaders outside! "Sir, aye Sir!" "Fall outside in formation!" "Sir, aye Sir!" "Platoon 104, attention! Right face, forward, march! Left, right, left, right, left. Platoon left, halt! (1, 2) Form for chow march!" Platoon 104 is in the chow hall and is eating. The DIs are discussing the storm that is blowing in the Atlantic. They know the importance of knowing its locations and wind strength.

At 1300, the red flag is up, and DIs are very cautious. The Battalion has passed the information down to all companies. The storm is now a hurricane. Platoon 108 has a history class. Platoon 112 has a first aid class. Platoon 104 has a class on the chain of command. At 1400, all platoons are in route back to their barracks. Before arriving back at the barracks, the black flag is flying. All three platoons receive the command route step.

The platoons are back and online. They have received head calls and are standing by for rifle drill. Platoon 106 SDI SSgt. McNair is teaching right shoulder arms. Right shoulder arms is a four-count movement. The drill period went pretty well.

The training schedule has been canceled due to the temperature. The temperature at 1500 is 99 degrees. The commanding General has ordered the Battalions to keep all recruits inside the barracks. Recruits will leave for chow or medical reasons only. The Series Commanders of series 104, 108, and 112 have called for a series meeting and are informing their series of what will happen if the hurricane continues on the same course; Parris Island is the bullseye. "Hurricane Tammy will be 200 miles off the coast of Parris Island at 2400," the Series Commander stated, "The wind strength will be 75 miles per hour. We are not planning on evacuation, but we will be prepared. When I dismiss you back to your barracks, the DIs will pack everything. Is that clear?" "Sir, yes Sir!" The series has sea bags back in their squad bays. The recruits are packing their sea bags. Recruits leave out their shaving bag, t-shirt, skivvies, and one pair of socks in their footlocker. Everything in the whiskey locker (supply closet) is being packed. The recruits have packed their linen, all except the wool blanket and pillow.

Their DIs have ordered the recruits to store everything at the rear hatch (door). It is still a black flag, and the temperature is 101 degrees. The hu- midity is 100% and holding. It is now 1700, and series 104 is going to chow. The series is now sitting on the First Battalion side. All the DIs are discussing the hurricane that is coming their way. They need to make sure their families will be okay. The series Gunnery Sergeant has recommended that they have their families leave as soon as possible. He tells his DIs that he has a funny feeling about this one.

Series 104 is back at the barracks. The SDIs send their DIs home to help pack their family belongings. By 2000, their families have left for their parents' homes. The DIs are back at the barracks and ensuring all is secured on the outside as well inside. At 2100 on August 2, 2021, the base is closed.

Hurricane Tammy moves northwest at 15 miles per hour; winds are steady at 75 miles per hour. At 2200, all recruits on Parris Island are prepar- ing to mount (go to bed).

"Mount!" Lights are out, and DIs are in their duty huts. The base Sergeant Major has called a meeting with all Sergeant Majors on Parris Island. The base Sergeant Major tells all the Sergeant Majors to ensure their Battalion area is prepared for the coming storm; 75 miles per hour is no laughing matter. The base will take care of all matters on the hurricane.

It is 0500 all the recruits are up on Parris Island. From base headquarters, all Battalions have been informed the temperature is 89. Parris Island has not been in this position before. The storm is still heading towards Parris Island. The chow hall has fed all the recruits on the island. At 0900, all the Marines and recruits were issued Meals Ready to Eat.

Hurricane Tammy is 140 miles off the coast of Parris Island. Tammy's wind speed has increased to 85 miles per hour. The DIs have continued training recruits in their barracks. They are teaching drills and teaching the classes the recruits have already had. At 1100 and it is time to feed the recruits again. The chow hall will continue to feed recruits until 1230. At 1300, all the recruits are back at their barracks.

The black flag is flying. The temperature on Parris Island is 105 degrees. Hurricane Tammy is 100 miles from her bullseye. Tammy has started to slow down. She again is moving at 15 miles per hour. At 1300, Hurricane Tammy began to wobble and came to a complete stop. Parris Island and Beaufort have been notified by the National Weather

Service about their situation. Hurricane Tammy will be hitting Parris Island around midnight. It is 1630, and the wind is gusting to 29 miles per hour. Rain is coming down like sheets. The evening meal will be MREs. Is Hurricane Tammy going to change course or what? The Base is aware of what Hurricane Tammy is doing. The base has the military police checking the entire base to make sure every Marine is inside.

It is now 2200 and all the recruits are in their racks. Hurricane Tammy has not moved in over 5 hours. The National Weather Service has posted a new report on Hurricane Tammy. She is moving and still on a course of Northwest. Her winds have increased to 103 (category 1) miles per hour. Her speed is increasing to 15 miles per hour. She has hurricane-force winds as far out as 50 miles. Parris Island should start to feel those hurricane winds by 0100 on August 3rd. At 0200, Hurricane Tammy was a category 3 storm. Parris Island is getting winds up to 100 miles per hour. The causeway is underwater, and a lot of the island is starting to flood. 1st Battalion has been ordered to move all the recruits from the first deck. That move has started. Everything is being moved to the 2nd and 3rd decks.

The company commanders have ordered that mattresses be put to the windows if the windows start to implode. Parris Island is feeling the winds of a category three hurricane. The 1st deck of all barracks are being flooded. The hurricane is now a category four hurricane with winds of 140 miles per hour. Parris Island is in trouble, and the hurricane is still 29 miles off the coast. The men inside the barracks can hear the wind as if they were outside. It is now 0800 and Hurricane Tammy has hit her bull's eye. Waves up to 6 feet are pounding the island. Windows on the bottom deck of the barracks are bursting, and the ocean is running in. Most of Paris Island has been flooded and will have to go through this for 3 hours. Parris Island is in dire trouble.

At 1700, SDI SSgt McNair went home and had a busy day with the recruits. He hears his wife Tammy crying and screaming, and he rushed into the bedroom. He is trying to wake her up. She is screaming, "The hur- ricane!" over and over. "Tammy, wake up, wake up!"

SALEM

I am Master Sergeant Larry McNair and I am about to retire from the Marine Corps. I am stationed in Okinawa, Japan. I am applying for an MCJROTC position. I put out several resumes. A few schools called and hired me over the phone. But the one that I liked was Salem High School in Conyers, Georgia. So, I flew from Okinawa, Japan, and interviewed with Lieutenant Colonel Jones for the position. Before I returned, they had called and told my wife Terri I had been hired.

Now how did I find out about MCJROTC? I was a Senior Drill Instructor at Parris Island, South Carolina. Platoon 2097 was out for Drill. Since I was out on the Drill Field, anybody and everybody could hear my Drill Instructors and me. The Privets were catching it from all of us. I would always look to see if anyone was watching us. I happened to look to my right, and off in the distance, I saw an officer. I turned the Platoon over to one of my Drill Instructors, Sergeant Moore.

I started walking towards the Officer. I could see he was a Colonel and much older. I reported to him, "Sir, Good morning, Staff Sergeant McNair, training day 21; I have 60 privets on deck Sir. He replied, "I am Colonel Miller, Staff Sergeant McNair, stand at ease. I am watching you teach the Platoon. I am not spying on you. I am retired, and I teach MCJROTC." "Colonel Miller, could you tell me a little about MCJROTC?" I asked. And he did. Well, that day planted a seed, and I knew this could be an op- portunity for me. This was December 1981, and eleven years later, I started my new career.

On July 20th, 1992, I left Okinawa with my family. We went to Shallotte, my hometown. A few days before I retired, I visited my family and Terri's family. It was very nice to be home and catch up on things. Terri and I had bought a van in Okinawa from the Marine Exchange. So we went to Jacksonville, North Carolina, to get it. The Dodge dealer had it ready, so all we had to do was get into it and drive away.

On July 27th, I left for Air Station New River, Jacksonville, North Carolina. I reported to Head Quarters Squadron and gave them my retire- ment orders. The Sergeant Major asked me if I wanted a retirement parade. "Sergeant Major," I said, "I do not want a parade. I have to report to my new job on August 5th."

On the morning of July 30th, I retired from the Marine Corps. It was a short drive back to Shallotte. That afternoon I left with Terri to find our family home in Conyers, Georgia. It was a six-hour drive; on arrival into Conyers, we found a Holiday Inn. The following day we went house hunt- ing. This was not easy, but on the 3rd day, we found the one we both liked. We drove back to Shallotte to get our children. We said, "See you later!" to our families, and we were off to Conyers, which is 15 miles from Atlanta. The owner of the home let me rent the home until we closed on the loan. We all slept on blowup mattresses. Before the end of August, our furniture arrived from Okinawa, Japan.

Salem High School was in its second school year. There were forty cadets in the program. There were no morning classes, and the first JROTC class was after lunch. In the mornings, I taught at Heritage High School with Lieutenant Colonel Jones. Now I was coming off active duty, and I was very loud. But right away, I let the cadets know that I cared about them. The Leadership course is an elective the students could take to graduate. I taught Marine History, Health, Public Speaking, Drill, and the Marine Uniform. Cadets were to wear the uniform one day a week. The day they wore the uniform, they received an inspection. It was the same as an active- duty Marine. All the uniform days missed had to be made up.

The 6th Marine Corps District inspected the programs once a year. Captain Hewitt was the Officer in charge of the MCJROTC program for the District. The inspection would not be easy. Cadets would spit- shine their boots or dress shoes. I had a percentage of cadets wearing all the uniforms we had in the program. 1st Platoon would drill in their cammies. The 2nd Platoon would stand the personal inspection. Both platoons brought their uniform to school to prepare them. I helped with Heritage and got them ready for the morning inspection. Heritage got a score of 97.5. It was out- standing! That afternoon, I prepared Salem for their inspection.

I had Salem for 90 minutes before the cadets would be inspected. I had them under stress because I believed it made them work better. The cadets were working very hard. I could tell they were excited and, at the same time, nervous. I worked better under stress. I felt I had to prove to the District that the cadets were in good hands. It was a challenge for the cadets and me. The cadets inspected each other, and I double-checked them. The cadets put on their uniforms and inspected each other. I was excited to show them off.

The personnel inspection went first. The Cadets did very well; they answered most of the questions Captain Hewitt asked. The drill platoon fell out. The entire program watched the drill platoon perform. The Drill Platoon performed very well. Captain Hewitt now had to add all his scores together and determine how well the cadets did. The cadets were sitting in the classroom. Captain Hewitt stood there and stared at the cadets. He was telling them they could have done better, but a 96.5 would have to do. I looked at the Captain. He said, "Job well done."

After Captain Hewitt left, I told the Cadets that the class leaders and all the Cadets working together made this happen. I was very proud of them. The program was very well-liked by the administration. Cadets would clean up the campus and field day (clean) the class once a week. I do not know if they did at home, but they did whatever the program needed. Class leaders would lead them in PT (physical training) once a week. Some of the Cadets were in good shape, but others needed improvement.

I had a female and male color guard. The male color guard, Cadet McNair, Cadet Briggs, Cadet Williams, Cadet Phelps, were going to do an Atlanta Braves game. They practiced three times a week until it was time for the game. Game day finally came, and they were ready. The Color Guard did an outstanding job. Cadet L. McNair, Cadet Williams, Cadet Briggs, Cadet Phelps will have a memory that will last them a lifetime.

Let me tell you about the girl Color Guard, Cadet Ward, Cadet Smith, Cadet Washington, and Cadet Long. I will start with moody, opinionated, emotional, but most of all, they were loyal. They had that determination that would not stop. They were preparing for a drill meet at the University of Tennessee at Chattanooga. They practiced after school five days a week— the practice lasted about two hours. Color Guard Commander Cadet Long motivated them at every practice. But she would correct them and tell them to get their s... together.

It was time for the Christmas vacation. As a result, the color guard would not practice for two weeks. My wife, Terri, and our children Larry, Corey, and Kristi had a great Christmas. We enjoyed our time together as a family. We visited our parents in Shallotte, North Carolina. Shallotte, where Terri and I meet. We have known each other since we were children. We opened our presents with both of our families. We just had a great time. But all good things must come to an end. We did not say goodbye; we said, "See you later."

When we came back for the Christmas break, the girls were a little rusty. The girls stayed longer and worked harder. There was harmony between them.

The night before the competition, I had a meeting with the girls' moth- ers. Mrs. Ward, Mrs. Long, Mrs. Washington, and Mrs. Smith. They were excited for their girls. Now the girls have been working on their uniforms in the classroom. They would be taking two. Their Dress Blues and their green slacks, khaki blouse (shirt), tab (tie), and their Wooly pulley (Sweater). Their shoes looked like corfram shoes, which only Officers and Staff Non- Commissioned Officers could wear. The girls spit-shined theirs to perfec- tion. We packed up my van with their uniforms, color guard equipment, and things needed for repairs.

We all would meet at the school at 0400. Everyone showed up on time. The mothers and girls were very excited. Once we got to Chattanooga, we would stop for breakfast. Cadet Long was telling her color guard that loser was not in our vocabulary. We discussed the day with everyone. They knew it would be a long day. When we arrived at the Coliseum, the girls got dressed in their Green Uniform. They were looking great, and they knew it.

It would be in the afternoon before they would perform. So, the girls let everyone know they were there. Cadets from other schools would stop them and ask about the Marine Program. The girls did not miss a beat. This day they got themselves well known. It was time for lunch, and their mothers wanted to take them out for lunch. I do not remember the restaurant's name, but it was worthy of a President. We all were very excited and ready for the girls to perform. But we would have to wait a bit longer. The girls would be the last Color Guard to perform.

They got dressed in their Dress Blues and walked around in the Coliseum. They were sharp, and the other schools knew it. It was finally time for them to perform. Many gathered around to watch them. They looked sharp in their Dress Blues. They looked like active-duty Marines. Finally, they re- ported to the head judge and got permission to perform. I cannot explain the moments, but I saw them with my own eyes. The girls nailed it. They reported out, and now we would have to wait.

The head judge started naming the schools that won 1st to 3rd place. He now was calling out the Color Guard winners. Okay, the girls did not take first, but second place. What a day! We came, we conquered, and we left. The girls were the talk of the program. I was very, very proud of them.

The school year was over. I had never been in this situation before. I had to find things to do, but things to do were everywhere. I went home to visit my family. That we did enjoy. I managed to get things done around our home.

At last the new school year started. I was glad to be around cadets again. The program numbers increased to 80 cadets. I welcomed all the returning cadets back and welcomed the new cadets to the program.

Rockdale County had three schools. Lieutenant Colonel Jones taught at Heritage, Master Sergeant Wilson at Rockdale, and I was at Salem. If any of the Salem cadets wanted to be on the shooting or the drill team, they would have to go to Heritage (shooting) or Rockdale (drill Team). I said that each school should have its own teams. That did not go well with Lieutenant Colonel Jones. But my cadets wanted their drill team, and I knew if I did this, I would have to look for another school. Salem did get their drill team, and I started looking for a new school. The new school did not happen right away.

I continued to carry out my duties at Salem. The year was going on like nothing was wrong. We were preparing for our annual inspection with the 6th Marine Corps District. The returning cadets started showing leadership by example. They would show the new cadets how to wear the uniform and how to spit-shine their shoes. They helped them with their knowledge. It was a pleasure to see them work as a team. Finally, the inspection day came, and the cadets did outstanding with a score of 95. Taking care of the campus and cleaning the classroom continued, and the school noticed the cadets.

The University Of Auburn was hosting a JROTC drill meet. The drill team would practice in the morning and after school. They were becoming a well-oiled machine. Lieutenant Colonel Jones was not happy, but he did not stop it. I could tell the team was tired of practice, but I told them they must break through that negative feeling. In a few days, I saw their motiva- tion was back. On the night before the meet, parents were briefed on the trip, and they signed the liability letter. There were many questions, but all were answered. The team packed everything that was going that night. The team was told to be at the school at 0430. We left that morning at 0500. The team was motivated, and it showed on their faces. We arrived on the campus with plenty of time to get dressed in their uniforms. They helped each other, and they looked great.

We had five Color Guards performing, and they were the first to go on. I thought they did perform well. The regulation drill team was to drill at 1400, and the time was 0900. The team got out of their uniform. They had four hours before they had to get back into uniform. The team watched their competition perform. After a while of seeing other schools perform, we had lunch and just laid around; some took a nap. It was time to get back into uniform. The team helped each other and inspected each other. I had the Platoon Commander warm up the team. I had my last little speech with the team, and I saw they were ready for this. I think I was more nervous than they were; Salem was to report to the Head Judge. Salem came to show that they were to be noticed by all the other schools.

The team marched on the drill area and reported to the head judge. The head judge had them carry on—people, I wish you were there. Did they carry on? Does a dog bark? I could not ask them to do any better. What a show the team put on! Before I knew it, they were marching off the drill area. Then all we could do was wait.

It came time to pass out the trophies. Salem took second place for the regulation Drill. The head judge started naming the top three teams. Salem took second place overall, now the reason why was because of our total score. We had five color Guards and a drill team. Our actual score was second overall. The color guards may not have won a trophy, but their scores did it for us.

MCJROTC has been in Salem for three years. The program has officers. I promoted several cadets to Cadet Second Lieutenant Cadet McNair, Cadet Briggs, Cadet Williams and Cadet Hardy. I did not ask Lieutenant Colonel Jones. Lieutenant Colonel Jones showed up on campus and was upset. I told him that I felt Salem, in many ways, was his stepchild. Lieutenant Colonel Jones left faster than he did when he arrived.

The next day I started looking for a new school. Since I was Navy Certified, I called Pensacola and asked if there were any openings.

"Yes, Master Sergeant McNair, Lithonia High School is looking for an enlisted Instructor." Lithonia is 15 minutes from my home. I called the school for an interview, and it was the next day.

At 1300 I was meeting with Principal Shaw. He asked me why I wanted to leave Salem for Lithonia. I told him it was just my time to leave. He kept asking me why and I finally gave him the answer. I needed more flexibility, and I wanted to be trusted more. The principal accepted my answer. He told me he was looking for a Marine-enlisted Instructor. Principal Shaw showed me the classrooms. I was okay with them. I thanked him for his time and returned to Salem. The following day the Principal called and congratulated me for being his choice and hired me for the next school year.

I called Lieutenant Colonel Jones and told him I was leaving. That afternoon he came to see me. When he arrived, I welcomed him aboard. The first thing he said to me was to sign this evaluation. It wasn't bad, but it wasn't the best either.

I read it and signed it. He asked me if I had any questions; then I an- swered his question with a question. "Yes, I do," I replied "Why are you so negative about this eval"?

Lieutenant Colonel Jones could not answer my question. I told him I had no hard feelings toward him. Lieutenant Colonel Jones told me I did not have to leave. We could work this out. I thanked him, and I also thank him for giving me this opportunity. We shook hands and said goodbye.

I informed the cadets I would not be returning next year. They all had their say that day, and our eyes dropped many tears. Salem cadets gave me a send-off party. It was outstanding. The only thing I hated about this send- off was that I had to speak to them for the last time. We said our goodbyes.

Over the years, I have seen many of them and seen how successful they are. Once a Marine Cadet Always a Marine Cadet. Semper Fidelis.

Ladon Briggs went to Salem High School. This story is dedicated to him.

LITHONIA NAVY JUNIOR ROTC

It is August 1994; the school year has started at Lithonia High School. I am excited to get started and to meet the cadets. I hope I will be up to the challenge this year. I do not know how to say what I need to say. But I will try; I hope I do not say the wrong thing around them. Lithonia is mostly a black school. I knew that before I applied for the job. But that did not matter to me. I was thinking about the culture; I now wanted to learn from it. I would have to learn before the cadets would trust me. I would ask the cadets to help me find my way. So, my first day, the Lieutenant Commander (LTCD) introduced himself and then me. I sensed the cadets were not sure about the program. There would be plenty of time for the questions. We had them introduce themselves. I could tell they were embarrassed to speak to strangers. I would be spending a lot of time on their self-esteem. Now a lot of the cadets knew each other. That was a good thing.

At the end of the first day, cadets were already dropping the program. The program is not for everybody. A lot of the cadets did not choose the program; their counselor chose it for them. We gave each class several forms to be signed by their parents or legal guardians and to return them in the morning. The principal assigned teachers different duties; I had the cafeteria. I stood it the first day of school, only nine more months of this fascinating duty.

Well, the first day was over. I had many thoughts going through my mind—good ones, not the wrong type. On my way home, I knew this school was where I belonged. My wife wanted to know how my day was. I told her it went well. I needed some time to myself, so I went into our sunroom. Before I knew it, I was sleeping. When I finally left the sunroom, all my family was in bed and asleep.

I left for work at 0630. I wanted to make sure everything was ready for the day. I had morning duty, which was to monitor the students getting off the bus. The principal had all the students go to gym to wait for the bell to ring for their homeroom. The bell rang, and the teachers directed the students out of the gym. I was in the JROTC classroom. The cadets came into the classroom, and they were quiet. I greeted them good morning. I had them stand up and say the Pledge of Allegiance. I could tell they were not used to saying it. I took attendance and sent the report to the attendance office. Then I explained I would teach the morning procedures.

First, I taught Attention, and from this position, they would repeat the pledge. Next, I taught the command At Ease. I told them they would call me Top McNair; I explained my rank was Master Sergeant, but Top would be accepted. They would not sit down until they were told to by one of the Instructors, and then I gave them the command Seats. I told them to hold up the forms they were to have signed. Not all had them signed, and I ex- plained it was vital that they are obedient to all orders. The Cadets would not be issued their uniforms until all forms were turned in.

I took them outside and put them into a formation. I explained what a formation was and what it was used for. Then I went over the position of Attention, Right face, Left face, and parade rest. We went over the move- ments several times. The period was ending, and the cadets changed classes. Every class was taught the same thing, and I would stand my duty in the cafeteria. Before I went home, the LTCMDR discussed the day and how he felt it went. I did not agree with him on every issue, but I kept silent. Finally, I left for home, and in my head, I went over the day and thought I could have done better.

It is 0630, and I am off to Lithonia High School. I arrived at about 0700 just in time to watch the students exit the bus. Nothing changed, so this will be the last time I discuss bus duty. It was time to issue the uniforms. The Commander was a lot of help.

I just fitted them as I would a Marine Uniform. And I had a tailor to help me. I thought they looked outstanding. The Tailor had the uniforms back in one week. The cadets tried them on, and to my surprise, they all fit. I gave a class on how to wear the uniform. The following Thursday was our first uniform day. The first time wearing the uniform, you will see everything and anything. It was hard to keep a straight face, but I stayed positive and corrected them.

We have been in school for two months. The Cadets are catching on and doing fine. The Lieutenant Commander told me I must wear a dress uniform to work. It would be the Charlie Uniform (green trousers, khaki shirt, and tie). I informed the Lieutenant Commander that would not hap- pen; I was wearing the camouflage uniform. He got furious and left the office. He went to see the Principal and told the Principal he did not have any decision-making on the enlisted Instructor. He wanted a Navy enlisted man. He also informed the Principal that Master Sergeant McNair would stop wearing the cammie uniform. The Principal called for me to come to his office. Like any good Master Sergeant, I reported to the Principal. He called me Sergeant all the time. It did not bother me.

"Sergeant, what is your side of this story?" he asked. I knew I had to watch my use of words. I said, "I interviewed for this job, and I was told by the retiring Principal he was looking for a Marine. The Commander does not like my choice of Marine uniforms. I have been wearing this uniform for 22 years, and I will not stop now." The Principal told me to go back to work, which I did. The Commander continued to find things wrong but had no luck. Then one day, he found a book on my desk.

He called me into his office, and he started! "I knew you were preju- diced!" he exclaimed. I said, "What in the hell are you talking about?" He picked up the book and waved it around like, 'I got you now!' "Lieutenant Commander, what do I do on Tuesday and Thursday nights?" He said, very sarcastically, "You go to school." "I am taking a Psychology class," I stated. The Lieutenant Commander just looked at me and said, "Larry, I am very sorry." I reached my hand out, and we shook hands. Two weeks later, he informed me he had been hired to teach in New Orleans. I really did not know what to say, but congratulations.

The Lieutenant Commander had been gone for about three weeks, and he called me at work. He told me he had convinced the Principal to hire me and pay all expenses. I was speechless but finally told him, no, and he understood.

The Drill Platoon had been practicing since the third day of school. I do not think I have seen anyone more interested in being the best drill team in their district. Lithonia is in Dekalb County, Georgia. Dekalb

County was holding a drill meet only for cadets enrolled in the 13 county schools. Lithonia had now been practicing for four months, and they are ready. The drill meet was being held before Christmas break.

The Friday night before the meet, I met with the families. I had them sign the release letter so the county would not be responsible although I know this form is not worth the paper it is written on. The parents were told what time to have their cadet at school.

The cadets loaded their uniform and shoes in my van. Rifles and all Color Guard equipment were also loaded up. I told the cadets to meet at 0700 at the school; the drill meet would start at 0900. We were to leave the school at 0730 but the school bus never showed up to take us to the meeting. At 0800, we started loading the cadets in the parents' cars and vans. The cadets had to get dressed there on campus. The cadets got dressed anywhere they could. They inspected each other; time was running out, we had to leave. We left the school at 0830 and arrived at the drill site at 0855. The cadets quickly got inside the drill area.

We immediately had to fall in for the Inspection. The cadets had inspected each other; they were ready. The Platoon Commander reported to the Navy Chief. When the chief stepped in front of a cadet, they gave their rank and last name. I watched their Inspection, and I was nervous, just like the day my wife gave birth to our first child. The Inspection was over, and the Platoon Commander gave the Command Platoon Fall Out.

The Commander asked me, "How do you think we did?" I just could not answer that question. I said, "We will find out later today." I had the Color Guard practice, so they would have their timing down. I was loud, and I was giving the Color Guard a little get-it-right moment. A Navy Chief came over to me and said, "Top, you are a new school. Do not expect that much from them this year."

That made me mad as hell. I pulled him over to the side so we could not be heard. I said, "Chief, I do not know what you think of your Drill Platoon, but I told mine, we are winners, and winners go places in this world. Losers are at the bottom of the totem pole. So, they choose to be winners." He left pissed at me. Oh well.

It was time for the Color Guard to perform. I just told them, "Do your best, and good things will happen for you all." The Color Guard Commander reported to the Head Judge; it was on. They performed like a well-oiled machine. They looked better than a Marine Color Guard. When they were finished, I just stared at them, and I was speechless. The Drill Platoon had to wait before they went on. We ate lunch and just relaxed. Now it is not easy to relax around me, but I really do not think they wanted to be relaxed. The cadets had Drill on their minds. Now I had been nervous since the time I got out of bed. I think I kept everyone around me nervous. Lithonia was warming up; they were making sure their timing was good. I wanted them to see me because I kept them thinking. I wore a red baseball cap with the Marine Logo. That hat is well known; the cadets looked for it.

The Judge was telling Lithonia to report in for Regulation Drill. My last words to them were, "Do what you have trained for." The Platoon Commander gave the command to fall in. I was watching, but it was hard for me. They nailed it; now let the fun begin. Some of the other schools were watching. Facing movements, you heard their heels click. They hit their rifles so hard you could hear it everywhere. Then the show even got better. They were on the march. Their heels were hitting the deck; it was music to my ears. Before I knew it, they were finished. Lithonia did not have an exhibition team (Fancy Drill), so we could not take first place.

At the end of the Drill meet, Lithonia took first place in the Inspection, Color Guard, and Regulation Drill. We finished second overall. I saw the chief that told me not to expect that much from them this year. I just smiled at him and said, good luck to your team.

The school year was coming to an end. Near the end, we took an orien- tation trip to Parris Island, South Carolina. I wanted the cadets to see what Marine Boot Camp was all about. We arrived aboard the base and went straight to Edison Range. This is where all the Recruits would qualify with the rifle. I was told to go to a particular barracks, and the Drill Instructors would be waiting for the cadets. We pulled up to their barracks. A female and male Drill Instructor were at the position of Attention. Before we left Lithonia, I told the cadets the Drill Instructors did not play and they had better listen to them. The vans stopped and the Drill Instructors ordered the cadets out of the vans. It had begun; all I could hear was, "Get in formation!

You are too slow; push-ups begin!" Finally I said, "Get on your feet! I said get in formation!"

The cadets were totally confused, but then suddenly, they remembered what a formation was. They were sounding off at the top of their lungs. The female Drill Instructor took the female cadets to their barracks, and the male Drill Instructor took the male cadets. The female chaperone went with the female cadets, and I went with the male cadets. They were going to teach them to count off and make their racks. The male cadets were moving faster than I had ever seen them move! They were using the 'sir' word and that motivated me. I wondered how the female cadets were doing.

The male cadets were working hard on the racks (beds). I had not heard a word come from the cadets. Their racks and rack displays were done. The Drill Instructor had all cadets in the same barracks. They were telling them what they expected from them. Still, I heard, "Yes, Ma 'am!" and "Yes, Sir!" and I just loved it!

The cadets fell out for Drill. Both Drill Instructors were marching them around the drill area. The Drill ended and the cadets were sent to the barracks to clean their hands and get back in formation for chow. They did not waste any time, and they were back in formation. This would be the first time the cadets had eaten in a Marine Chow Hall. Both Drill Instructors got their details in a single file. They grabbed a tray and sidestepped down the chow line. The cadets were directed to their tables and told to sit down.

"You have twenty minutes to eat and get back in formation," the cadets were told. They took these Drill Instructors seriously. Maybe they were not hungry. Well, the cadets were now back at the barracks. The Drill Instructors told them they'd see them bright and early in the morning. The cadets showered and shaved and brushed their fangs. They had already started to tell war stories. The girls and boys were just sitting around and doing what teenagers do on a Thursday night. I really didn't believe that they were making sure they'd be ready for the Drill Instructors in the morning.

The female chaperone took the girls back to their barracks, and they all are ready for lights out. I was tired and ready also to hit the rack. Good night, Chesty, wherever you are.

It is 0430, and the Drill Instructors are in my duty hut asking if they could hold a low-stress wake-up call. I said, "Yes, but very low, and please let the chaperone know what you are doing." 0500, the lights come on.

Thunderous voices are yelling, "Get out of those racks!" The female cadets are still half asleep. "That's right, take your time. You ladies are too slow so get back to your racks. Too slow! Do it again!" Finally, they moved fast enough to satisfy the Drill Instructor. The male cadets were greeted with a perfect morning, one that they will not forget. All cadets received head calls (bathroom). After the head call, they got dressed and outside for morning chow. They marched over, and they were looking good. The drill Instructors lined them up. The cadets were in the chow line and side stepping through it. The Drill Instructors told them, "If you take it, you will eat it." They were hungry and took it all. When they started to get up, one of The Drill Instructors told them to stay in their seats and eat their chow. When chow was over and the cadets were in formation, the Drill Instructors told them to clean the barracks and get ready to watch a Recruit graduation. The Drill Instructors welcomed them to Parris Island.

At 0745, the Cadets went to watch morning colors. (Raising the American Flag) After Colors, the cadets walked to the parade deck to watch the gradu- ation. The cadets enjoyed it very much; after the graduation, we said our goodbyes.

We arrived back in Lithonia, and the parents picked up their cadets. I told the cadets I was proud of them and that they represented Lithonia High School well. The school year came to an end. I would teach one more year before leaving for Okinawa, Japan. The cadets taught me that love has nothing to do with the color of skin. It is all about the heart. May God Bless and keep you safe, Lithonia.

PAULA ALICIA IS ONE PERSON I WILL NEVER FORGET. SHE WAS THE DRILL TEAM COMMANDER. , SHE WORKED THE DRILL TEAM HARD BUT SHE WAS FAIR

BETTY BELL WAS THE DRILL TEAM MOM. SHE TOOK CARE OF THE DRILL TEAM FROM THE TIME THEY LEFT SCHOOL UNTIL THE TIME THEY GOT BACK. IF THE UNIFORMS NEEDED REPAIR, SHE DID IT. BETTY WAS A TREMENDOUS HELP TO THE DRILL TEAM.

STEWART CLINTON WAS IN THE PROGRAM FOR FOUR YEARS. HE WAS THE DRILL TEAM COMMANDER COMPANY COMPANY COMMANDER AND THE BATTALION COMMANDER.

ERIK F. AGE 35, OF LITHONIA, PASSED AWAY APRIL 20, 2015. ERICK WAS IN THE PROGRAM FOR FOUR YEARS. ERICK WAS A MEMBER OF THE DRILL TEAM. MAY HE REST IN PEACE.

Kubasaki Marine Corp Junior Rotc

It is August 1996; the McNair family is on their way to Okinawa, Japan. We are so excited to be returning. We had lived on the Island before while I was on active duty. The military bases on the Island are very accom- modating. I will be teaching MCJROTC at Kubasaki High School. The school system is the Department of Defense Dependent

Schools. We are leaving Conyers, Georgia; we have sold our home. Our household goods are on their way to Okinawa.

Department of Defense Dependent Schools (DODDS) sent our Passports and reservations. DODDS did all the necessary paperwork to get us to Okinawa. Before leaving, we were home visiting with our parents. We enjoyed our time with them. I went fishing with my father. We ate with my wife's family tonight. We enjoyed the dinner and the time we had with them. But time does not stand still, and we must leave.

That day came; our families were at the airport to see us leave. It was a sad moment. We left from Wilmington, North Carolina. By the time we arrived in Okinawa, we had been traveling for 24 hours. Major Sam Smith, Kubasaki's Senior Marine Instructor, met us at the International Airport in Naha. We had a perfect welcome to Okinawa. Major Smith knew we were tired, so he took us to our hotel, the Hamagawa Lodge in town, where most Americans stay temporarily when they arrive. Major Smith would pick me up at 0900 in the morning.

My family and I did not sleep well because of the jet lag. Early in the morning, I found a family mart (convenience store). I got breakfast for the family. Terri and the kids tried to sleep, but it was a hit-and-miss thing. About 0830, I got into my uniform and waited for the Major. Major Smith was on time. He took me to Kubasaki to check in. After checking in, we went car hunting. I found one that I liked, but Terri would have to like also.

Major Smith took Terri and me to the commissary to pick up a few things. On the way back to our room, I showed Terri the car. She liked it, so we bought it. We could not pick it up until it had its Japanese Inspection. We also had to get our driving licenses. The next day Terri and I did just that; we got our driving license. We rented a car on Camp Foster. On Okinawa, you drive on the left side of the road. I was a little nervous, but I have driven on Okinawa before. Two days later, we had our car.

We moved into a house on Camp Foster. It had three bedrooms, a bath and a half, a study, a living room, a dining room, a small kitchen, and a laundry room. It was five minutes from my work.

School started on the 28th of August, and I was ready. On the first day of school, Terri needed the car to go to the Exchange. She took me to work. Terri said she would pick me up at 1630.

Major Smith greeted the Cadets. He introduced himself and welcomed the cadets to MCJROTC. Then he introduced me. It was a great introduc- tion. Major Smith turned over the class to me.

Master Sergeant Jones had left. The cadets were unhappy with his de- parture. I know Master Sergeant Jones was vital to all of them. I hoped I could fill his shoes. I could tell this was going to be a minor problem for me. Terri was on time to pick me up, and she said, "How did it go?" I told her all about it, and then I just started laughing.

The second day of school, I met Cadet Ward. He was the Supply Officer. I was explaining to him how I would like the supply room arranged. He disagreed with me and said he would not comply with my request. I in- formed Cadet Ward that it was not a request. It was a damn order. I told the Cadet Ward to leave from my sight and hurry. Cadet Ward went to Major Smith. He told him I was changing too many things. "Major Smith," he said, "could you correct the Top so he won't make the changes?" Major Smith told Cadet Ward he would obey the Top's order. Cadet Ward left the program. It was best for him.

That day, I had the opportunity to get to know the Cadets. They gave me their names and what grade they were in. Before the end of each class, I would meet again with the officers and staff noncommissioned officers. Major Smith and I had our meeting. We both agreed that some Cadets would be a little sad because they had lost Top Jones.

On our third day of School, a Typhoon was approaching Okinawa, so schools on the Island were closed. Typhoons would visit the Island often. We would sleep, and Terri would read a book.

The next Monday, we were back in school. The cadets are ready to go. I give them a class on Marine Corps history. To each cadet, I pass out paper so they could take notes. During the last ten minutes of each class, I had the Cadets compare their notes.

The Navy Criminal Investigative Service informed me I was under investigation. They would not tell me why I was being investigated. Well, this made me mad as hell. I went over to their office. When I started to ask questions, they clammed up. Where, when, who claimed I did some- thing? They asked me to leave, told me at no time would they discuss an ongoing investigation. I wanted to tell them to kiss my ass. Major Smith was informed that he also was under investigation. I asked Major Smith if he knew why? His answer to me was no. I was on the Island for less than a month, and this happened! What in the hell was going on? I told Terri; she was also confused. What were the charges? That night I was thinking about the investigation. Do I have a future at Kubasaki?

The cadets had drill the next day. The Company Commanders and First Sergeants taught the movements. I wanted to check their knowledge of close-order drills. The company Commanders were not at the level I ex- pected them to be. The cadets were okay but not at the level I was expecting.

I reminded every class to bring their Pt gear with them in the morning. That would consist of shorts that would not make a sexual statement: a green T-shirt, tennis shoes, and white socks. Major Smith and I had a meeting. He thought everything was going okay. The investigation did not come up. I left for home and just went over the day in my head.

When I got home, I asked my lovely wife, Terri, if she would like to go out and eat. She just stared at me like, are you crazy? Of course! Okay, let's go to the NCO Club, it has excellent food. Our two children tagged along with us—Corey, a freshman at Kubasaki, and Kristi, who is in the 3rd grade at Kadena Elementary. We had a great dinner at the club. Our oldest son,

Larry, who was in the Marine Corps stationed at Quantico, VA, has now retired from the Marine Corps. He and his wife and family live in Honolulu.

It was PT (Physical Training) day. When the cadets came into the classroom, they changed their clothing. The girls changed in the shooting range. The boys stayed in the classroom. The Cadets were dressed, and it was time to take attendance. The cadets went to the soccer field for a motivating PT session. The Company Commander cadet Lowe led them through their exercise movements. Then he led the cadets on the run. At last, PT was over, and the cadets showered and dressed. I reminded all the cadets to wear the Cammie uniform on Thursday.

On Thursday morning, some of the cadets were not in their uniforms. I had them call their parents to bring their uniforms to school. I could tell this was something they were not used to. When the parents got to the classroom, they were not happy. One parent challenged me in front of his cadet. I said, "GySgt, are you not in uniform?" That was the end of that discussion. The Inspection Day went okay. I hoped the cadets knew that I was serious about them wearing the uniform. The cadets had been told if they missed three uniforms days during a semester, they would fail. Every time they missed the uniform day, I would have them call their parents. Parents got tired of bringing in uniforms.

On Friday during class, I had the cadets take an object out of a box. Then they had to speak for five minutes about it. It became an exciting event. Some cadets had a great imagination. Some spoke about its true meaning while others struggled. It had been a good week overall. The investigation was still active. I did find out that it was something that happened last year. Stupid, why am I being investigated? I was not here last year.

The drill team started to practice. I noticed that they were not drilling at an acceptable level. The Drill Team Commander, Cadet Bryan, told me practices would start until one month before the Drill Meet. I got the team together and told them the past is the past. Kubasaki is the future of Drill.

Practice would be every day after school until the extracurricular bus leaves. When the other schools think about Drill, they would think of Kubasaki.

Christmas break arrived. The cadets were excited and had been looking forward to Christmas. Terri had been shopping, and the presents are under our lovely tree. We got the tree from the Exchange. It was a pitiful-looking tree! I had to tie it to the wall to prevent it from falling. We still laugh about that lovely tree. During the break, I made sure all the cadets' paperwork was correct. I ordered some uniforms and I did some maintenance on our rifles. The program uses the M14, which is an excellent Drill rifle. I enjoyed my Christmas break with my family. We had time to see the Island again. It reminded us how pretty the Island was.

We started a new semester. I welcomed the new and returning cadets to MCJROTC. The annual inspection was coming up. The 12th Marine Corps District, from San Diego, California, would be the inspecting com- mand. I told the cadets, this will be the most challenging thing we have done this year. The personnel inspection would be held in the cafeteria, and the pass-in review would be on the school soccer field.

The cadets were working hard to get the inspection right. I was applying stress on them. When they were in class, and when they made mistakes, I gave pushups and many other physical movements. I did not have the entire program practicing at the same time. So I did every practice as though they were. The pass-in review was a mess. The cadets were having trouble with the officer's center. I am sure they will get it right.

The Drill platoon is showing a lot of improvement. Our Drill meet is in two weeks. I am on them like stink on poop. The team is going to meet our goal. I understand they are in high school, and they are not Marines. I am teaching them that life sometimes is problematic. They must suck it up, and remember we are Kubasaki MCJROTC. This program will achieve all our goals.

It is the day before the drill meet and the cadets are spending the night in the MCJROTC building. I have a female chaperone, Mrs. Hawkins. The female cadets are in a different part of the building. The team drills for a short time. Parents have brought in their dinner. The platoon did the last inspection of their uniforms and all their equipment. Before I put them in their rooms, I took them by surprise. I was calling them by their names. Cadet McNair, Cadet Harper, Cadet Duncan, Cadet Jesus, Cadet Ryan, Cadet Simsome, Cadet Johnson, Cadet Hewitt, Cadet Kilkenny. They all looked at me and said, "You do know our names!" We had a good laugh! Now you must go to your sleeping area and try to sleep. Well, I know that's like telling a dog not to bark. I slept in the same classroom as the boys. I did not sleep well. Neither did the cadets.

We were up and eating breakfast. After breakfast, we held a quick clean- up and packed all our gear. The cadets loaded the vans with their uniforms and equipment. We arrived at Kadena High School and fell into formation for the opening ceremony.

After the opening ceremony, the shooting teams started their competition. The Kubasaki shooters are Cadet Rayan, Cadet Hewitt, Cadet Killkenny, and Cadet Johnson. This year, nine teams are competing.

The shooting continues up to lunchtime. After lunch, all the schools go on a short break.

The teams get dressed for the drill portion of the meet. At 1300, Kubasaki's color guard reported in and got permission to perform. The Color Guard started their routine. I was nervous but managed to watch them. The Color Guard was performing like a well-oiled machine. I knew they had won. "Cadet McNair, Cadet Duncan, Cadet Johnson and Cadet Hewitt, you four looked like winners." The Color Guard was hungry, and they ate.

The head judge called for Kubasaki's regulation drill team. The Platoon Commander Cadet Bryan reported to the head judge. The Platoon Commander had control, and the team was performing well. I cannot put it in words, but all I can say is "Wow!" The team finished their routine, and nine of Kubasaki's' best left the drill area. The other schools were talking and watching Kubasaki.

Kubasaki had to prepare for the uniform Inspection. We had lint re- movers and everything we needed to prepare for this inspection. Kubasaki was ready, the head judge called for Kubasaki to report. The team fell into formation. The Platoon Commander Cadet Bryan reported to the judge. The Inspection was now in progress. The cadets were catching hell from the judges. The cadets were sounding off loud and clear. The nine cadets did not lose their bearing, Kubasaki impressed me.

The Exhibition drill team was warming up. (Fancy Drill) The schools were coming from everywhere. The big event was about to happen for Kubasaki. The drill team had practiced this routine since the beginning of school. Kubasaki reported to the Head Judge. I just told them to knock their socks off, "Give them hell, boys!" The platoon was performing the eight- minute routine, without commands. I am not going to attempt to put it into words. When they were finished, the schools clapped forever, it seemed.

It was 1600, and the awards ceremony did not begin until 1900. Kubasaki left for the MCJROTC classroom on Camp Foster. The team took off their uniforms and were getting some shut up, close eyes and mouth time. By the way it is my favorite game.

We were off to the unknown. We arrived at the Kadena Officer Club. Kubasaki went to their assigned seats. Everyone ate an outstanding dinner, and all the schools enjoyed themselves. Well, the unknown was about to become known. The officer from Kadena, Lieutenant Colonel Borris, spoke to all the Cadets, telling them how he has enjoyed having them at Kadena this year. It was time to present the trophies—Color Guard third place Seoul, second place Zama, and first place Kubasaki. Next up is the Shooting—third place Yokota, second place Seoul, and first place Kubasaki. Next up was the Inspection, third place Kinnick, second place Taegu, first place Kubasaki. Next up was Regulation Drill, third place Kadena, second place Zama, first place Kubasaki. Next up was Exhibition Drill (Fancy Drill), third place Seoul, second place Kadena, and first place Kubasaki. The overall winner is Kubasaki. Lieutenant Colonel Borris thanked all the schools for coming, and said, "We will see you again next year." Lieutenant Colonel Borris did not pass out the trophy for the overall winner. I asked Lieutenant Colonel Borris why he did not give Kubasaki the overall trophy. His answer was, "Just grab it." I wanted to tell him to kiss my ass.

When we returned to Kubasaki, the cadets went straight to the classroom. They were on a natural high. I joined them in their celebration. Kubasaki was the first school to sweep all events. Parents started showing up and joined in the celebration. I looked at Major Smith, and he had a giant smile on his face. The cadets left with their parents, and my family also went home. Major Smith did his regular thing. It was Friday night.

Sunday morning, I took my family to the Butler Officers Club. The club serves a great brunch. You can enjoy breakfast or lunch. You can have both if you like. After breakfast, we went to the Camp Foster Exchange. It has a great choice of things, and the Mall has a lot of local businesses. Corey and Kristi enjoy shopping. Terri took all of us home because she was not finished with her shopping. She enjoyed shopping at PHAI'S House of Jade.

The cadets were working hard preparing for the extensive inspection. The Administration let all six classes practice at the same time. It was a little shaky at first, but they got it together. Now the cadets understood.

The investigation into Major Smith and I had not been completed. My son told me the investigator who spoke to him asked some very embarrass- ing questions. They talked to all the cadets. I do know the family that went to the NIS.

The two cadets were still in the program. I talked to them often, but I said nothing about the investigation. I even know the alleged charges.

When will this come to an end? I do not know why they are investigating me. I was not teaching at the time of the allegation. Master Sergeant Jones was here with Major Smith.

I had the cadets bring in their uniforms, which they were going to wear for the inspection. The tailors checked them. If the cadets had gained or lost weight, I tried to fit them with a uniform in the supply room. The tailors found uniforms that needed tailoring. The tailor returned and the cadets looked great in their uniforms. Finally, all uniforms fit the cadet core. The program has three weeks to prepare for the Inspection. The cadets continue to work on their uniforms. This is a very stressful time in the program. If the cadets can handle me, they can handle anyone. I am a believer in atten- tion to detail. I teach all the cadets they must dot there i's and cross their t's. Kubasaki will be ready for this Inspection. I know they are high school students, but they are in a leadership course. Some of the staff think I am too hard on them. I say that's a joke. If it is easy to achieve something, it is probably useless. This inspection teaches the cadets teamwork, pride, unity, and self-esteem. I believe that I am teaching them how to handle real-life situations.

The Company Commanders are showing their leadership skills. The First Sergeants are leading all Staff NCOS and ensuring they stay on top of their NCO'S. Kubasaki is looking good and on schedule.

It was the night before the Inspection. I picked up Captain Baker and Mr. Brown. I welcomed them to Okinawa and I took them to the Hamagawa Lodge. I told them I would pick them up at 0700. I did not sleep well; my mind was on the Inspection. At 0600 I was up and drinking a cup of mud (coffee). I kept telling myself they were ready; damn it, they were ready. I left to pick up Captain Baker and Mr. Brown. They were waiting for me outside. I informed them the cadets would dress in the MCJROTC building.

The cadets were dressing and moving to the cafeteria. Then the cadets were in the cafeteria for information. When Captain Baker walked in, the

Battalion Commander Cadet Ryan called the Battalion to attention. The Battalion sang the Marine Hymn. Each Company sang a different verse. It was so motivating! The Battalion Commander Cadet Rylan reported to Captain Baker. Captain Baker inspected the Battalion Commander Cadet Rylan and his Staff first. Each Company stood at the position of At Ease. When Captain Baker was approaching the ALPHA Company, the Company Commander Cadet Hewitt called his Company to Attention. Captain Baker inspected all the cadets. The Battalion Commander Cadet Rylan Called the Battalion to Attention. Captain Baker briefed the Battalion Commander on his findings. After the briefing, the Battalion Commander Cadet Rylan saluted the Captain. Captain Baker did an about-face and marched off. The Battalion fell out to the soccer field For the Pass in Review. The Pass in review was outstanding. The Battalion was briefed by Captain Baker. He was very impressed. The Cadets had their best day of the year. Major Smith told the cadets he was very proud of them. Captain Baker briefed Major Smith and me, and he thought the program looked outstanding. I was glad that this was over, and the program could get back to teaching.

Major Smith and I were informed that the investigation was completed. The inspectors found nothing wrong with either of us. This had been an exciting year. It had its crazy moments, but that's life.

We received a phone call from Mr. Brown that the program was not selected for an Honor School. He said we were close. There were five schools selected. Major Smith thanked Mr. Brown for the phone call. We told the program the news, and they were very disappointed.

The following week, Mr. Brown called again and informed Major Smith that Kubasaki did make Honor School. You could hear the Major all over the Building. I went down to the Major's Office, and he told me the good news. Major Smith asked the school office to announce it over the school intercom. The cadets heard the excellent news! This was the first time Kubasaki was selected to be an Honor School.

The school year came to an end, and I was very proud of the cadets. I feel like I gained their respect. I would miss them over the summer.

JENNY HERRIN WAS IN MCJROTC FOR FOUR YEARS. SHE WAS
100% DEDICATED TO THE PROGRAM. JENNY WAS A MEMBER OF THE
SHOOTING TEAM. IT WAS A PLEASURE HAVING HER IN MY CLASS.

This short story is in memory of Private First Class Juan Velasquez. I had the privilege of teaching Juan. He was so dedicated to the program. Until we meet again, once a Marine always a Marine. Semper Fidelis

OKKODO

My Name is Larry McNair, Master Sergeant United States Marine Corps, retired. I will be interviewing for a Marine Corps JROTC position. Okkodo High School is opening a new program. It is in the village of Dededo on the island of Guam. Dededo is known as the little Philippines. The people of this community are great.

The interview will happen at 1630. The time on Guam is 14 hours ahead of the Eastern Daylight Time. The main road is Marine Drive, which goes north and south. It connects the Air Force and Navy Base.

I am standing by for the phone call. My phone is ringing, and I answer, "Hello?" I hear, "Is this Master Sergeant McNair?" "Yes, it is," I reply. "I am Mr. Denusta, the Principal of Okkodo High School. I understand you are certified by the Marine Corps to teach JROTC." "Yes, I am Mr. Denusta." "That is great to know. Tell me about yourself," he said. "I am married to my lovely wife, Terri. We have three children, all grown." "What do you think about living in Guam?" he asked. "Sir, I do not know that much about Guam, but I do like island living." He asked, "If you are hired, what will you offer the students?" "I will teach them how to respect others. Nothing is free, be a better citizen, and patriotism," I replied. He said, "I want Okkodo to have the best JROTC on the Island. Can you do that for the students?" "Yes, sir, I can, and I will." "Do you think we could have a winning Drill team?" "Yes, sir, and I will have a winning team this year!" "I liked your answer," he stated. "You have impressed me. Master Sergeant McNair. You will receive a letter stating you have been hired to teach MCJROTC." "Thank you, Sir!"

I arrived on the Island on June 16th. The Guam Department of Education met me at the airport. I had an excellent welcome to Guam. Mrs. Cruz gave me a ride to Avis to rent a car. It did not take long, and I was off to the Naval Station. I had a reservation for a room at the Navy Lodge. A very pretty young lady was working at the main desk. She checked me in. When I left her desk, she greeted me, saying "Haifa Day" (good morning). Unfortunately, jet lag kept me up most of the night. My body was so tired! It would take a few days for my body to adjust to the local time.

The following day I drove to sign all the paperwork for my position at Okkodo High School. Everyone was so kind, and again I heard "Haifa Day". I was signing all my admin papers. I noticed a problem with my salary; they were fifty thousand dollars short. I made it clear I would not work for that salary. Mrs. Santos told me they would correct it. I thanked her and greeted her saying Haifa Day. Later that day, Lieutenant Colonel Williams, the Senior Marine Instructor, and I met each other. It was a good meeting; we both had questions about each other. I found out that this was his first school.

Mr. Denusta showed us our classrooms and supply room. I could not believe what I was seeing! The best JROTC facility I had ever seen. I was going to enjoy all this space. Mr. Denusta was excited that we were happy with the MCJROTC space. Mr. Denusta told us that the construction shop would build racks to hang the uniforms on. The racks would be built before the school year got started. I went over to the construction shop and intro- duced myself, and thanked Mr. Velasquez. He also welcomed me to Guam.

Liberation Day would be on July 21st. Mr. Denusta said he wanted our cadets to march in the Parade. I looked at Mr. Denusta, "Sir, the uniforms have not arrived." He laughed and said, "That is your problem!" I told him the problem was in good hands.I suggested black trousers, a red pullover shirt, and a red hat. Mr. Denusta, still laughing, said, "I need their sizes; the school will purchase them." The program would march ten Cadets in the Parade. The Cadets would practice at 1000 the following day.

The Cadets showed up on time. They greeted each other and just happy to see each other. The Cadets knew how to fall in. Last year Okkodo, started the program without the Marine Corps' permission. Mr. Denusta was sure they would approve it, so why wait. Major Jones at Headquarters in Quantico, Virginia, told me that Mr. Denusta jumped the gun. I laughed, and I thought to myself, 'Who is this man, Mr. Denusta?' So the program had a foundation. Cadet Sanchez was the Platoon Commander. He did know his left from his right. I put the cadets into two squads to practice at school. The cadets were informed they would practice every day until the day of the parade. The parade went well and I was proud of the cadets.

Thursday was the first day of school. The LTCOL introduced himself and then turned the class over to me. I introduced myself and gave the class- room rules. I informed the male cadets that they would get their haircuts at school. "I have already spoken to the barbers," I told them. You could have heard a pin drop. Cadet Florez asked, "What style will we get? Do we have a choice?" I smiled and looked at him straight and said, "You will, and your choice will be high and tight." The Cadets looked at Cadet Florez, and they had a good laugh. All six classes got the same information and forms their parents must sign to be issued their uniforms.

Lieutenant Colonel Williams and I had a meeting before I left for the Navy Lodge. I asked Lieutenant Colonel Williams where he was staying. He told me he was staying at the Hotel Nikko. I asked him if he would consider the Navy Lodge, and he said yes. So, he called the lodge and got a reservation. We both thought that the day went well. We were on our way to the Navy Lodge. It is at the southern end of the Island. We stopped at the convenience mart and picked up something for dinner and breakfast. The jet lag still had us both. I hoped I would sleep better tonight.

Friday morning has arrived, and the Cadets had their paperwork signed and turned in. Lieutenant Colonel Williams and I started to issue the Cammie uniform. The Cadets were so happy to try on the Marine uniform finally. All six classes were issued a Cammie uniform. Thursday would be the first time the Cadets wore the uniform. Some of the Cadets have been waiting over one year.

After work on Friday, I started looking for an apartment. I had a real estate agent, Mr. Blas, show me several apartments. Mr. Blas showed me the apartment I thought my wife Terri would like. It was in Tumon, a lovely community. The apartment was behind the Catholic Church. Tumon is where all the resorts are; Tumon is beautiful. The beaches are amazing!

It is now Saturday morning, and I am moving into my apartment. I had a blowup mattress because our furniture has not arrived yet.

Lieutenant Colonel Williams was moving in until he found an apartment. Tuesday, I will pick up my cars from the port. After school, Lieutenant Colonel Williams would go with me.

Monday morning, I took the role. After taking the role, we said the Pledge. Cadets did the morning procedures. I gave a class on Marine Corps history. I passed out a paper to help them take notes. Near the end of the class,

I had them check each other's notes. All six classes received the same class. Battalion Commander was Cadet Sanchez, Battalion Sergeant Major Cadet Benavente, A Company Cadet Acosta, B Company Cadet Cruz, C Company Cadet Flores, D Company Cadet Camacho, E Company Cadet Nelia, F Company Cadet Eriuos first Sergeants A Cadet Kihleng, B Company Cadet Castigador, C Cadet Sakiwo, D Company Chochol, E Company Smith, F Company Cadet Kaipat. The Cadet core now had a chain of command. First, the Cadet Sergeants picked their squad leaders. Then the squads were all in a line and their desks covered down—each Company had three Squads.

After school, the moving company delivered my furniture. So I must, and I would have Terri's apartment looking fantastic.

Tuesday after school, we are on our way to pick up my cars. I have a Ford Focus and a Dodge Durango. When I saw them, I was happier than a pig eating slop. It was nice to have a car again. I let Lieutenant Colonel Williams drive the Ford Focus until he got a car. During the weekend, we both did different things.

Today is a special day; my wife Terri will arrive. Terri will arrive at 1800 at the Guam International Airport. I arrive early. They say the early bird gets well anyway. The plane is on time, and I see my lovely wife. I gave her a big kiss, and it seemed like we hugged forever. I got her luggage and I took her to our apartment. I open the door, and she goes in before me. She loves it. Our furniture looks good in her new home. I had groceries waiting for her.

Monday morning, I am back at work. The classroom procedures were done. "Cadets, take your seats. Cadets, we are going to learn how to master Drill. Drill is the essential tool the Marine Corps has to establish discipline. When executing a movement like right face, you are obedient to order. That is discipline. Now all Marine drills have two counts. The first count is the Preparatory Command. It tells you what you are going to do. Like 'right,' you are doing something to the right. The second count is when the movement is executed. You execute on the face. For the remainder of this period, we will work on stationary movements, which means you are not marching. We will work on right face, left face, parade rest, about-face, and at-ease."

I have started the drill team. Several cadets showed up today. All the cadets heard my do's and don'ts. There are more don'ts than do's. Practice would go after school, Monday through Friday. "Here is a permission form that a parent must sign," I explained. "I want them back tomorrow. Bring something comfortable to practice in, but do not make a statement with what you are wearing."

Lieutenant Colonel Williams gave a class on the role of an officer. I would work in the supply room. All the uniforms had to be hung up, with the hanger facing the same way. The shirts and trousers and slacks legs needed to drape the same way. The men, and lady's shoes, toes would be the same way—socks, t-shirts, ties, and tabs on the shelves. Dress blue coats are hanging the same way. Dress coats (green) are hanging the same way. I will have a detail to help me with the supply room."

September, a busy month and cadets are preparing for the Marine Ball. The drill platoon will be the Honor Guard, Color Guard, and Cake Detail. The youngest and oldest Cadet will come from the Cadet Corps. Our ball will be in Tumon at the Plaza Hotel and Resort. We practice for our ball after school for thirty minutes, then go to drill practice, five days a week and sometimes on Saturday. Our ball practice is going well. The cadets are excited about the ball. The ticket price for the ball is twelve dollars a per- son. Lieutenant Colonel Williams and I are shooting for three hundred and fifty people. There are five other schools in Guam with JROTC programs. Three Army, one Navy, and one Air Force. We have invited 20 cadets from each school.

Ball practices have been going now for eight weeks. Okay, I know that is a long time. The Marine Ball will be on November 10th, the Birthday of the Marine Corps. Mr. Denusta and his wife Aileen will attend, along with the Assistant Principal Blas and his wife Ann, instructors from the five schools, and other staff members.

Our Guest of Honor will be Colonel Smith, Commanding Officer of the Marine Detachment Guam. I have ten days before the ball. I must pay at the Hotel Plaza three days before the ball. Time is running out. Am I missing something? All the Cadets have paid and their guests. Mr. Denutus and his wife are Honored Guests; their dinners are free. The Guest of Honor Colonel Smith and his wife's meals are also free. Cadets are busy making seat assignments. The Cadets and their guests have made their choice of meals: chicken, beef, and fish. The Plaza Hotel is making the birthday cake. I think I am ready to celebrate the 234th birthday of the United States Marine Corps.

I am paying for the ball today: I have a check for $4,050. While I was paying for the ball, the manager showed me the cake, which was outstand- ing. The Cadets know all the rules, what to wear, and the time the ball will start and end. Parents must pick them up by 2330. The night before the ball, the Cadets set up the VIP room—tables 1 through 29 on the starboard side and 30 thru 58 on the portside. The cadets were assigned a table. Tables one through five will be for Honored Guests. The Cadets know what table they have been assigned and will look for their tables during the social hour. I have assigned a cadet to the VIPs. They will greet them and escort them to their table.

Finally, it was November 10th, the day my Marine Corps came alive. I arrived at the Plaza one hour before the ball. The VIP room is looking great. The scarlet tablecloths and the gold napkins are the official colors of the Marine Corps. Lieutenant Colonel Williams has arrived with his wife, Tammy. They are at table one. The social hour has begun; cadets and their guests are looking for their tables. Cadets can have their pictures taken at this time.

At 1800, my wife Terri arrives. She is escorted to her table. At 1830, the Guest of Honor, Colonel Smith, and his wife Teresa arrive. Both are escorted to their table. At 1840, Mr. Denusta and his wife, Ms. Aileen, are escorted to their table. The Narrator, Cadet San Nicklas, has announced the ten-minute warning, and to please be seated. "Five-minute warning, please be seated, turn off all cell phones. One minute warning, please be seated and turn off all cell phones." The Guest of Honor and cadets and their guests are at their tables. Okkodo's Narrator Cadet San Nicklas reads the Commandant's message.

The Ball Adjutant, Cadet Capt. Jones takes her position, and draws her sword. Then she gives the Command, "Sound Attention!" The Marine Corps Band sounds the first Attention. The Honor Guard is called to Attention. Sound Adjutants call The Band, which marches forward, then does a coun- termarch and marches off the floor. The Adjutant follows the Band.

Once the Band takes their position and seats, there is a second sound. The Honor Guard marches on two at a time. The other Guard members are marking time. The following two step off, then the next two, and finally the last two. They halt, then face left and right, take four steps forward, do an about face, then they lower their swords. All of this is done with preci- sion. After the Honor Guard has marched on the third sound Attention, The Cadet Battalion Commander Cadet Sanchez and the Guest of Honor Colonel Smith march on and take their positions. On the fourth sound Attention, the Color Guard centered on the Commanding Officer Cadet Sanchez and Guest of

Honor, Colonel Smith, then stopped. Everyone is still standing. The fifth Sound Attention then sounded. The Color Guard Commander Cadet Hannagan gave Present arms.

The Ceremony is at Present Arms. The Marine Colors are dipped on the first note of the National Anthem. The Color Guard Commander gives the command, "Order Arms!" On the last note of the Anthem, the Marine colors come to their ordinal position. The Color Guard Commander Cadet Hannagan gives, "Countermarch, March! Forward, March, Countermarch,

March! Color guard halt! Order Colors, post." The six sound Attention, then the Marine Hymn was played very slowly while the cake was marched on. Behind the cake was the oldest and youngest Cadet. The cake was then halted and the cake detail posted. The Cadet Battalion Commander Sanchez marched to the cake. He is handed a sword. The song Auld Lang Syne was played while Battalion Commander Cadet Sanchez sliced two pieces of cake and put them on two saucers. The Guest of Honor, Colonel Smith, received the first piece, took one bite, and returned the saucer to Cadet Battalion Commander Cadet Sanchez. The second piece was given to the oldest Cadet, who took one bite, faced and handed it to the youngest Cadet, who took one bite, and returned the saucer to the Battalion Commander Cadet Sanchez. This part of the ceremony represents the passing of tradition from generation to generation. Finally, the cake detail marched off.

The Color Guard then came to the position of Attention. They side-stepped to reform, and the Color Guard Commander Cadet Hannagan gave the order, "Carry Colors! Forward, March!" while the song "Semper Fidelis" was playing. The Color Guard executed a countermarch and then forward, march. The Cadet Battalion Commander Sanchez ordered, "Forward, March!" for him and the Guest of Honor. Once the Guest of Honor passed the first two of the Honor Guard, they carried swords, then marched to the center of the floor, halted, faced left and right, and stepped off. Then it was like a ripple effect until the Honor

Guard was off the floor. The Band played "Anchors Away," and then came the "Marine's Hymn." Everyone was at the position of Attention. The Narrator then said, "Ladies and Gentlemen, please be seated and enjoy your Marine ball."

The Guest of Honor would give his speech after dinner. The dinners are being served to the Guest of Honor and his wife first, then the other honored guests, then the cadets and their guests. I have eaten my Birthday meal. I move around and talk to the Cadets and their guests. I see a lot of parents have come. I stop and talk to our visiting Cadets. They are impressed with what they have seen.

The Cadet Battalion Commander Cadet Sanchez introduced the Guest of Honor, Colonel Smith. His speech started with, "Good evening Mr. Denusta and Mrs. Denusta, Lieutenant Colonel Williams and Mrs. Williams, and all Cadets and parents in attendance tonight. It is a great honor that I have the opportunity to speak to you. I am looking at America's future, and if tonight is any indicator, America is in good hands. This is your first year. This program has marched in the Liberation Parade and is now celebrat- ing the Corps Birthday. Unfortunately, I do not think that MCJROTC Headquarters is aware of your enthusiasm. You wear the uniform with pride, and I can tell you are proud of the uniform." The Colonel continued to speak, and we who heard it were proud to be a part of this night and the program. He ended with, "Thank you for inviting me to Okkodo's first Marine Corps Ball." Colonel Smith receives a standing ovation. The Cadet Corps dances until it was time for the ball to end.

The next day all the cadets were present for school. All six classes talked about the ball. They all said this memory would last a lifetime. Classes con- tinued, and the program was getting known on the Island. The cadets are helping with Toys for Tots. They would be at Kmart Saturday and Sunday at the Mall. The cadets were on Christmas Break. During this break, I had Color Guards go to Mr. Denusta's Christmas programs. The cadets would continue helping Toys for Tots up to December 21st. The Salvation Army would also have a few cadets helping with the passing-out of toys.

School was now back in session. The cadets would field day our class- rooms (clean). The supply room was a little disorganized, but the Cadet leadership would make this happen. The Drill team was back at practice. They were rusty; they really stank! Okkodo would be hosting a Drill meet during February. There was going to be a total of four teams attending. Okkodo had one month to get their act together. So they were now practicing for six days. I was on them like stink on poop! Practice was very stressful, but I told them they know how I am.

I will not lose. Loser is not in my vocabulary. I have talked with the team. The team understands the situation we are going through. Mr. Denusta has attended some of our practices. He says nothing, but he is observing every movement. I promised Mr. Denusta when he hired me; we would be the best Drill team in Guam. The team had finally begun to look like they were hungry. A team with a mission, and that mission was to be the best.

I was and am very proud of this Drill team, my love for them, I can- not put it in words. I have told them many times that I love them all like a father loves his children.

The night before the Drill meet, the team made the last adjustment, working on their uniforms. They would wear the Dress Blue and Dress Blue white trousers. They knew to be in at 0600 on Saturday morning. That morning, the team was in and setting up the Drill area. The team had done a tremendous job on the drill area; it looked great. By 0730, the schools started showing up. Each school had a classroom for dressing. Each team had a cadet from Okkodo to assist them. Okkodo is now in their Dress Blue uniform. I had some cadets looking them over.

The judges were Navy enlisted men and women. The head Judge, Chief Moore, met with all the instructors and asked if they had any questions. The Instructors had none and were ready to start the meet.

At 0900 all teams had information for the opening ceremony. The National Anthem played, and all the cadets showed the proper respect. The head Judge introduced himself and his Judges. Chief Williams asked the Commanders if there were any questions, and there were none. The first event was the Regulation drill. John F. Kennedy HS (Air Force) is the first school to perform their drill. They were looking good and working hard. They left the Drill area, and the judges finished their score sheets. Cadet Blas from Okkodo took the judges' sheets to the Cadet classroom to be added up and put into their folder. The second school up was Father Duenas HS (Navy). The team was on the Drill pad and looking sharp. They were well prepared. When they finished their routine, the judges gave their sheets to the Okkodo runner. The scores were added up and put in their folder. The next School was Southern HS (Army). They were on the drill pad and wow, they were looking outstanding! Then Southern finished their routine and the judges gave their sheets to the Okkodo runner. The scores were added and put in their folder.

Finally, the last school was Okkodo HS (Marine Corps). The home Drill Team was ready. They are decked out in their Summer Dress Blues (white trousers) and marching better than an active-duty Platoon. Wow, they are looking good! The head Judge Chief Williams gives the Okkodo runner the sheets. The scores are added and put in their folder.

All four events have been finished. The schools are standing around, under tents because it is hot in Guam. The average temperature is 87 de- grees. Okay, this is true; Okkodo won all four events. Therefore, they are the overall Champions! The official standings are 1st Okkodo, 2nd Southern, 3rd John F, Kennedy, 4th Father Duenas.

After the drill competition, the parents of Okkodo served a barbeque. It tasted like, well, you should have been there. Mr. Denusta approached me, and he said, "You keep your promises." And all I could say was, "Thank you, Mr. D."

It had been an excellent school year and I hated to see it come to an end.

NOREEN WAS A STUDENT OF MARINE CORP JUNIOR ROTC FROM 2009 - 2012

Mr. Ken Denusta passed away February 13, 2020. He was Okkodos's first Principal. I enjoyed working for him and will always hold a special place for him in my heart. Mr. D, thank you very much for allowing me to teach the most fantastic kids on this earth. I dedicate this short story to this wonderful man.

THE DREAMER

It is a lazy Sunday afternoon. I just ate lunch and I am relaxing in my recliner. I love to reminisce on my past life. I taught MCJROTC for twenty-one years. I am retired now with many hours a day just to think about the cadets. I know I will go off to lala land and dream about those days. You know how lazy you feel when your belly is full? My eyes are getting heavy. I just want to sleep.

"Kubasaki, the schools we must pay attention to this year are Okkodo, Lithonia, and Salem High School. It will not be easy beating them. I understand they have very experienced instructors. We need to stay on top of our game. As usual, practice will go after school and there will be a lot of practices on Saturday. Be prepared to hear me get loud and sometimes I may seem rude."

It's a beautiful day on Guam. The Okkodo MCJROTC drill team is practicing for the big event. Master Sergeant (Top) McNair is working them pretty hard. The team cannot do anything right. "You guys need to get your heads out of your ass. Get your mind on what we are doing. Kubasaki, Lithonia, and will crap on us."

"Lithonia, what in the hick did you just do? Get your brain out of your butt. Cadet Clinton, tell me where your brain is today. Cadet Clinton, did you leave yours at home? Drill team, this is going to be a long month."

"This is a lot of bull! Salem, do you realize who we are taking on this year? Kubasaki, Okkodo, and Lithonia have great drill teams. They are preparing for us. They want to put us to rest. Rest! I do mean rest! As in the past, their Marine Instructor, MSGT. (Top) McNair is not a pushover. He will make us look like amateurs!"

Cadet C. McNair worked on the forward march and to the rear. Then a few column movements. "Kubasaki, we need a simple adjustment. Kubasaki! Pushups begin! Run in place! Pushups! Stop! Let's do it again." Cadet McNair gives them fall in. "I want you to watch their alignment. Do not drop your left arm before the cadet to your right has dropped their arm. My grand- mother could drill better than this. I want you to take the names of the cadets who are at practice. I need to pass out permission forms. McNair I will want the forms back tomorrow. Kubasaki will be the best drill team this year. I will not be easy on you, but I will be fair. Cadets, you know me and my personality. Come tomorrow prepared to become champions."

It has been a long day. I am very tired. I need some time to myself. That is always hard to find. The cadets are always needing some help with something. I am looking forward to going home. I think I will stop at hot wings and surprise my wife, Terri. They have the best wings I have eaten.

At 0632 I am in Okkodo. I have the best job a man could have. The cadets have a heavy schedule in front of them today. It is 1500 and the drill team is out for practice. Today we work on stationary movements. "Cadet Horry, let's get this practice going. What is wrong with your voice?" I stopped him. "Horry, where is your command voice? Get it together so the team can hear you. Now the team is marching better. What the hell did I just see? Give me some pushups. Stop! Fall back in and get your mind on what you are doing."

Salem did not have school today but the drill team is in. Cadet L. McNair is the platoon commander. "McNair, let's work on column move- ments today. I am concerned about the alignment and cover." The drill team is marching and they look like crap! "Stop! Where is your mind? We cannot complete looking like this. I know your level of drill and you are below it. I have seen all of our competitors and they are very good. On the video, Top McNair is a hard ass but he is fair. Tomorrow, promise yourselves you will have a better day."

It is 1800 and I am preparing to go home. My body is telling me to rest. I arrive home and Terri has my supper ready. Good old fried chicken! (Redneck food) Larry Jr. is not home; he has a part-time job at Burger King. It is his gas and girlfriend's money. Corey and Kristi are doing their homework and being brats towards each other. Home is where I charge my battery for the next day.

At 0630 Lithonia is ready for another day. I walk the campus and I make sure it is safe for the students. 0730 and the cadets are ready to start their day. Attendance has been taken by the company commander and all cadets are present. "Cadets in class today we will discuss responsibility. My question to you is, "Who is responsible for you?" I heard mom, dad, the community, and finally the right answer was given to me. "The cadet is responsible for himself or herself." "Yes, yes you are responsible for everything you do or fail to do."

At 1500 Lithonia is at drill practice. "Cadet Clinton, we are going to work on our exhibition today. We really need to drop some time from the routine. It cannot be more than eight minutes. We are at nine minutes. We will only have an eight-minute routine. Cadet Clinton is going through the routine and he has an idea. "Why can't we shorten the report out?" Clinton, that sounds good to me. Make it happen." "Okay Top."

"Practice went well today, cadets. I expect more days like this. If we are to win this meet, we must drill even better than today." I promised my family I would meet them at Ryan's family restaurant. The family was waiting on me. We all went in together. I opened the door for my wife and she went in first. Yes, I am a Southern gentleman. We had a great supper and enjoyed the family time together.

Okinawa is a pretty island; I enjoy living here. The people are so friendly and well mannered. It is 0630 and I am at Kubasaki. I will inspect the ca- dets today. They are in their cammie uniform. First period has started and all the cadets are in uniform. The inspection went well and I have a few minutes before drill practice. I need some chill time before practice starts. I know the team is outside fooling around. They need to let some steam off.

Cadet Mcnair lets us work on our exhibition routine. I want the team to go through the routine from start to finish. I timed the platoon below eight minutes and that is good. I think the platoon needs a five-minute break. Five minutes usually gets extended to thirty minutes. We all needed it. McNair has the regulation team fall in.

I said, "March them and work on the rifle movements. We need to make sure their arms are parallel to the deck and their elbows are locked to their sides on line with their back." McNair checks to see if they have their thumb and first finger in the shape of a donut. Cadets, I think practice went go but I expect more from you." I leave practice I think it is 1830. I am taking my lovely wife to the NCO club for supper. I am enjoying their seafood chowder; it is the best soup that they serve at the club.

We have one week before the drill meet. It is in Daytona Beach, Florida. I think my team is ready to compete. The team has made all arrangements to go to Daytona. I will stress them out this week. I will stay on their butts

like stink on poop. I am having a meeting with the parents tonight. I have forms that they must sign. "Parents, I want you to hear the rules for this trip. The female chaperone will take care of the girls. Her room will be next to the girls' rooms. The doors to all rooms will be left open until lights out. I will have no mercy for the cadet that breaks that rule.

Parents all their meals are paid for. The only money that they will need is up to you. I plan on taking them to Disney World. That takes money and more money. As soon as we arrive at our rooms your cadet will call you. Parents, this is not a vacation. Our mission is to compete in a drill meet. Our days will be long and with only two things on our minds. That is drill and safety. We leave this Monday morning; I need your cadet at school at 0430. School buses will take us to the airport. Are there any questions? Have a nice evening."

Salem, Lithonia, Okkodo, and Kubasaki are preparing harder than ever before. I keep them on their toes. I will not let them think they have already won this drill meet. The principal asked me what to expect. I said only time knows. I did not want anyone to know what my thoughts were.

It is Monday morning the parents have their cadets at school. The cadets have loaded the bus with all our gear. The cadets said their goodbyes to their parents. We are on our way to the airport. This will not be easy to get all of us and our gear through customs. At 0730, we are waiting at our gate. It was time to eat, so we found a fast-food stand and made our orders. I send the cadets to a table I pay for each of us. I think we all are in a better state of mind since we have something in our stomachs.

We are airborne; this will be a long trip. We arrive in Jacksonville, Florida. We have all our gear and our bus is waiting on us. Daytona, here we come and I will be glad when we get there. We have arrived at the Daytona Hilton and have checked in. All the cadets have put their suitcases in their rooms. The female chaperone is ensuring the female cadets have their doors open. Cadets have been told no visitors in their rooms until the next day. I have all the rifles and all the drill gear in my room.

Salem, Okkodo, Lithonia, and Kubasaki are in the restaurant downstairs. They are enjoying their breakfast. Top McNair had them back at their rooms preparing for drill practice.

Salem has found a place to practice. I am not happy with them, and they know it. I take them back to their rooms and lay into them. "Get your jet-lagged selves together! Cadet McNair, you will get them squared away!"

Okkodo is outside and is having big time problems. Cadet Horry has problems marching them. The jet lag has him under control. I am so pissed and they know it.

Lithonia is slow to get outside. They are already on my bad side. "Cadet Clinton, get their asses back to their rooms and play my favorite game, SHUT UP!"

I have Kubasaki at a place we have been before. They are very sluggish and have a bad attitude. The jet lag blues, I will keep them out here until they show me something. "Cadet McNair, you know how to get under my skin. Get these jet-lagged cadets away from me and now!"

I have them right where I want them and that is confused. I know by the third day we will be back and cooking with gas. We feed the team sandwiches and get them back outside. They need to keep working. It will help them with the jet lag. Practice is tough on my team. I keep reminding them why we are here.

It is the third day and the team is looking better. They are starting to hit the rifle with force. You can hear their heels hit the pavement. That is music to my ears.

It is Friday evening and Mr. Smith is having a meeting with all the schools. He runs and owns the company that puts on this meet. He has passed out the dos and don'ts. Each school has their schedule. We know now what time we will perform each event. I returned to my room. I called a meeting with the team. They now know our schedule for tomorrow. I send them back to their rooms, to make sure there gear is ready. I informed them that tomorrow will be a long day. We will be getting up at 0400.

I have them up and preparing to go to the event. I have paid for a private dressing area. It is 0600 and the doors are open. The team is in our room. I have the girls get dressed first. Now it is the boys' turn. The team is check- ing each other to make sure they are looking their best.

At 0700 the color guard is ready for their thing. Someone taps me on my back; I turn around and he says, "Are you Top McNair?" "Yes, I am Top McNair." "I have heard so much about your program!" "Marine, thank you very much." "Well good luck to Salem, Okkodo, Lithonia, and Kubasaki," he said. "Thank you and good luck to you." I thought to myself he looked very familiar.

Someone is shaking me, "Dad, wake up, it is time for supper." When I opened my eyes, my daughter said to me, "Were you dreaming?" I just smiled and thought to myself, was I?

This story is dedicated to my sons Larry McNair Jr and Corey McNair. Who were on my drill teams at Salem and Kubasaki.